# Christmas at Whisper Beach

## Also by Shelley Noble

# *Christmas at Whisper Beach*

## A WHISPER BEACH NOVELLA

**SHELLEY NOBLE**

*wm*

WILLIAM MORROW IMPULSE
*An Imprint of HarperCollinsPublishers*

An excerpt from *Whisper Beach* copyright © 2015 by Shelley Freydont.

CHRISTMAS AT WHISPER BEACH. Copyright © 2017 by Shelley Freydont. All rights reserved. Printed in the United States of America. No part of this book may be used or reproduced in any manner whatsoever without written permission except in the case of brief quotations embodied in critical articles and reviews. For information, address HarperCollins Publishers, 195 Broadway, New York, NY 10007.

Digital Edition OCTOBER 2017 ISBN: 978-0-062685698
Print Edition ISBN: 978-0-062685704

*Cover design by Nadine Badalaty*
*Cover photographs: © DenisTangneyJr / GettyImages (path); © scarletsails / GettyImages (wreath); © Jan Homolka / Shutterstock (sky)*

William Morrow Impulse is a trademark of HarperCollins Publishers. William Morrow and HarperCollins are registered trademarks of HarperCollins Publishers in the United States of America and other countries.

FIRST EDITION

17 18 19 20 21 OPM 10 9 8 7 6 5 4 3 2 1

*To families everywhere*

## Chapter One

VANESSA MORAN PRESSED her hands into the small of her back and stretched. Five huge boxes were left to unpack and it was already after three. She dragged another box into the storeroom and reached for the utility knife.

Someone knocked on the front door. "Yo, Van, are you in there?"

"Back here, Suze," Van called back.

The front door closed, footsteps sounded across the wooden floors and Suze Turner appeared in the doorway to the storeroom. She shrugged out of a fire-engine-red cargo coat and tossed it on the floor. Her hat and gloves followed the coat, leaving her tall, large-boned figure clad in harem pants and a "Nevertheless, She Persisted" sweatshirt.

Van held up her utility knife. "You know, when they

let you intellectual types out of your ivy-covered towers, we never know what to expect. 'Yo'? Really? Is that what a PhD in English gets you?"

"I'm practicing my vernacular. And stop waving that weapon around. I came to help."

Van frowned. "Really?"

"Really. Chaucer was getting me down and it's too early to declare happy hour, so I came to see what's up."

"Drag that box in here and I'll tell you."

Suze looked behind her and hoisted the box. "Heck, what's in here?"

"Either pine cleaner or wood-floor oil."

"Hmm," Suze said and took the utility knife. "I have to say, the old homestead is looking better than I ever thought it could."

"It does. Thanks for convincing me to use it for head-quarters instead of renting that overpriced, chic hole-in-the-wall on Main Street."

"See, us intellectual types are good for the occasional pragmatic morsel." Suze lugged two large containers out of the box.

"Second shelf on the far right."

"You mean where all the other ones just like these are?" Suze put the bottles next to the others and reached for two more.

"Sorry, I'm in micromanaging mode and I didn't have a victim until you came in."

"Thank heaven for ivory towers, imaginary people and the past." Suze lifted out two more bottles.

Van laughed. Suze never ceased to amaze her. They'd been best friends since they'd both had summer jobs working at Dorie Lister's Blue Crab restaurant down on the boardwalk. Van, still in high school, worked out of necessity. Suze, already in college, was willing to wash dishes, waitress, scrub floors—anything to avoid commuting to the city for an internship in the financial district.

When Van's future unraveled, Suze had literally saved Van's life. They'd lost touch until the past summer when they both returned to Whisper Beach for a funeral. It was meant to be a several-hour-long trip, but it had turned into something much longer for both of them.

Van was still doing manual labor but now for her own business. Suze was on sabbatical from Princeton, working on a paper entitled "Misogyny in the Works of Chaucer."

Give Van manual labor any day.

A few minutes later, the cleaning supplies were shelved, the boxes were broken down and Van and Suze were sitting in the newly painted kitchen waiting for the kettle to boil.

Suze got down two newly purchased mugs from the refaced cabinets. "You know it's amazing how much you've accomplished in a few short months."

"Between my Whisper Beach peeps and the crew from Manhattan it was a piece of cake. Now I just have to hire an office manager, a receptionist and cleaning and maintenance staff."

At first Van had been skeptical. She'd planned to expand Elite Lifestyle Managers—Organization for Families on the Go—from Manhattan to Boston or Philly. But her life had taken an unexpected detour and so had her business. Now her first branch office would soon be opening in Whisper Beach.

"You have time," Suze said.

"At least I decided to wait until after Christmas to open. Van looked around the room. "Can you imagine trying to get this place ready in the next few days?"

Suze grinned. "Me? No, but by taking an extra couple of weeks, you can enjoy the holidays and still be ready to capitalize on all those New Year's resolutions."

"Exactly," Van agreed.

The kettle whistled and Van poured water into the mugs. "I've only got generic tea. I was waiting for the new fridge to arrive before I stocked the kitchen, then I just got too busy and forgot. I do have milk and sugar."

"And nary a biscuit in sight," Suze intoned.

"Nope, but Joe's mom insisted I have this so I don't succumb to hunger while I work." Van took out a plate covered in foil and placed it on the table.

Suze pulled off the foil. "Mom Enthorpe's date nut bread. I'm in heaven."

"She said I was too skinny."

"It's just your metabolism. Now me on the other hand . . ." Suze's sentence trailed off as she cut into the date nut bread. She pushed the plate toward Van. "I shouldn't be eating this." She took a bite. "Hmmmm. This would be even better with cream cheese."

"Sorry."

"So how are you doing living at the farm?" Suze shuddered. "With Joe's parents."

"Actually it's kind of great. They're wonderful and we live at the back of the house. They made up a little suite of rooms for us, a bedroom, sitting room and our own bath."

"Nice. I still can't believe you moved out of Dorie's. Is this going to be permanent?"

Van cut herself a slab of bread. "I don't know. Yes. Maybe."

"Oh goodie, more vacillation on the same old theme. You know, you worry about stuff that hasn't happened more than anybody I know. If it doesn't work out, you do what thousands of other divorcees do . . ." Suze grinned. "You start all over again."

Van rolled her eyes. "That isn't Chaucer."

"Jerome Kern. Very smart man."

"I couldn't marry Joe knowing that I might bring him unhappiness."

"Pick yourself up, brush your . . ." Suze sang under her breath. "Just because you can't have kids doesn't mean you both can't be happy."

"I know. I just don't trust that it will turn out that way."

"You also never thought you'd come back to Whisper Beach. As I recall you were waffling between selling this house and burning it to the ground. And now, voila, you've transformed it into a dyn-o-mite, upscale, cutting-edge business office."

"Dana helped."

"Dana? What did I miss while I was hunkered over my laptop?"

"When she heard I was thinking about repurposing the house back in September, she made me burn sage in all the corners and doorways."

"Ah, to ward off evil spirits. Well, it worked. I don't feel anything but good times ahead."

Suze reached over to squeeze Van's wrist. "Seriously, the past is done. Only people like me dwell on it, and I get paid to do it. Look to your future, girl, and take the plunge."

Suze was right, except one part of Van's past had changed her future forever.

"Or we can talk about my future."

Van frowned. "Is something up?"

"Another dead horse we need to beat. I think I'll have another little sliver." She reached for the plate. "Dorie's feeding me like I was the prodigal daughter. Every time my mother sees me, she reminds me that her annual holiday please-marry-my-daughter party is coming up and she certainly hopes I'll be able to fit into my new holiday dress. Which by the way, I haven't bought yet."

"Oh," Van said. "I thought maybe it was Chaucer that was getting you down."

"Nah, medieval misogyny is a walk in the park compared to my mother's cocktail parties. I'd rather publish *and* perish than face her without a date."

"What happened to Jerry? He's always been willing to go with you."

"Alas he has to work. Being a cop at Christmas is not for the fainthearted. Besides, I'm beginning to feel a little guilty about always taking advantage of his altruistic spirit."

"You guys have a fight or something?" Van asked.

"Not at all. But we're just friends. That's all it's ever been. We make each other laugh. But there's no future there. I'm going back to Princeton when my sabbatical is up.

"Besides, outside of laughing, we have nothing in common. Don't get me wrong—he's a great friend, but he's a beer and football kind of guy, which I totally get, only I'm a white wine spritzer and British drama kind of girl."

"And ne'er the twain, huh?"

"Hey, you used to yell at me for saying that."

Van shrugged. "Just saying."

"Anyway," Suze continued. "I'm afraid hanging with me is—and I use the phrase loosely—'cramping his style.' I've noticed he's been hanging around Dana lately."

"Dana Mulvanney?"

"Do you know any others?"

"No. One is enough."

"True, but while you've been busy reconnecting with

Joe, starting a new business and overhauling the Enthorpe winery, Dana has been attacking her new life with a vengeance and turning the restaurant around. I swear she's a born-again, efficient business type—totally organized . . . Well, as much as a recovering Goth can be. You've been crazy busy lately. You wouldn't recognize her."

"I've been meaning to come over but it's just been so hectic between the office, the vineyard and commuting to the city every few days . . . Not to mention trying to build some kind of relationship with Joe while living with his parents."

"Yeah, I could see where that last part might be challenging for a longtime loner like you."

Van made a face at her. "Tell her I promise to come over right after the holidays. You're all still coming to the party?"

"With bells on. If I survive the *madre*."

"So who are you going to take? Do you want me to ask Joe?"

"Thanks, but I would never put him through that. Plus it would never fool my mother. Maybe I'll just tough it out this year. Who knows? Maybe I'll meet the accountant/dentist/financial advisor/podiatrist of my dreams there."

"Well, you don't have to have a date for the Enthorpe's party."

"Excellent. Still planning to hold it in the vineyard's new gift shop?"

"Absolutely. It's perfect. Once we gutted it and pulled down all the 'improvements' and stopgap fixes that had been made over the years, it was all original stone and rustic wood. I couldn't ask for better ambiance if I paid for it." Van sighed. "Still a lot of work to do."

"I have no doubt that it will be finished, organized and looking like a million bucks. You're a multitasking wonder. Just try to have a little fun while you're at it."

"I intend to."

Suze pushed her chair back. "Well, I'd better get back to Geoffrey C. Poor man. He lived in the fourteenth century. How was he to know that one day there would be feminist academics picking his *Canterbury Tales* apart?"

Van accompanied Suze to get her coat, waited while she bundled up and walked her to the door.

"You'd better pack it in soon," Suze said. "It's beginning to look a lot like snow clouds up there."

Van laughed. "I've never been around you at Christmas before."

"If I could carry a tune, you'd be amazed. But no kidding. Go home."

"I'm closing up in a few minutes. We're decorating the Christmas tree tonight." Van felt a familiar stab of panic.

"First family tree?" Suze sighed, then grinned. "Enjoy every minute of it, that's an order."

"You're so smart," Van quipped. Suze might have her head in the literary clouds, but she was the most insightful person she knew. At least into what made Van click. "It's all so, I don't know, Hallmark-y."

"And you're afraid the warm fuzzy bubble will burst?"

"No, well, maybe just a little. I don't know."

Suze laughed loud enough to shake the snow from the clouds. A couple of tiny flakes floated past them. "You'll be fine, but maybe you better brush up your 'Jingle Bells' on the way home."

Van watched Suze drive away in her old VW Bug— an odd spectacle of big person and little car. But they seemed perfect together and, according to Suze, the old car gave her a certain cachet on the Princeton campus.

Van stepped back inside and closed the door. With Suze gone, without her laughter and personality to fill the corners, the old house seemed too quiet. And memories she'd managed to ignore all day began to flit in the shadows.

She'd spent the first eighteen years of her life here and she'd sworn never to return. And yet here she was. She'd thrown out every stick of furniture, repaired and painted the walls, even let Dana exorcise any lingering evil spirits. She still got an occasional whiff of burnt sage.

Van laughed, a dim shadow of Suze's confident, luxurious belly laugh. Dana had been the bane of all their lives and now she was smack-dab in the midst of them again. Life was weird.

She checked the stove, turned out the lights, turned the thermostat down to fifty-eight. No reason to keep pumping heat if she wasn't going to be here for a few days. She had plenty to do back at the vineyard.

Most of her Christmas shopping was done, and wrapped. Employee bonuses had been distributed. Business holiday cards and gift baskets sent weeks before. There were a few last-minute presents to buy. A new holiday dress would be good. And Christmas carols to remember.

She did remember Christmas all those years ago. The Enthorpes singing carols, their voices raised in unison or harmony, on key or off, clear or husky, sopranos, tenors and basses making a joyful noise.

Sitting next to Joe, his voice clear as he smiled down at her like they would be there together, happy ever after. Van almost afraid to make a sound, hoping with all her fragile, abused heart, that it was true.

And when the singing wound down, Maddy stayed at the piano and sang "In the Bleak Midwinter."

And Van thought it was the saddest song she'd ever heard.

But this year would be merry. Merry and bright. A jingle bell Christmas. Her first Christmas since all those years before.

She grabbed her jacket, zipped it up. Gathered her laptop and folders into her briefcase and headed for . . . home.

## Chapter Two

"So, what do you think?" Joe Enthorpe asked. "Too big?"

Beside him twelve-year-old Owen Davis shook his head. "No way. It's dope."

Joe nodded.

*Dope* was Owen's highest accolade and something Joe still had trouble remembering was a good thing. The first time he'd said it had been at the Enthorpe dinner table and Van had just passed him a platter of fried chicken.

Owen's eyes had rounded. "That's so dope."

Joe's mom froze holding a bowl of string beans. His father and grandfather stared. Even Joe frowned. Not Van.

"Totally agree," she said. "Mom Enthorpe's chicken is the best. You want a leg, a breast or a thigh?"

And that was one of the many reasons he loved her.

While the rest of them were figuring out that that *dope* meant amazingly cool, Van had served Owen and herself and handed the platter to the next person. No lengthy explanations, just took it in stride and made sure everyone else did, too. Being a Manhattanite—at least for now, though Joe had other plans for that, too—she was up on the current slang.

"I think it's the most perfect Christmas tree I ever saw," Owen added, his mouth open and his face tilted almost at a right angle to see the top.

Joe nodded. It *was* pretty perfect. And he felt good about the day's work. The other Joes—his granddad Joe Sr. and his father, Joe Jr.—had announced that they were turning over the cutting of the family tree to the younger generation. So Joe had taken Owen out to the woods to find two trees, one for the house and one for the future Enthorpe Winery gift shop, which they were trying to get in shape in time for the annual Christmas party.

Of course, Owen wasn't an Enthorpe, but since Joe had hired him to help at the marina last summer, he'd practically been adopted by the family. He came out on Saturdays to help Joe with chores. Joe paid him for his time and Joe's mother, who everyone called "Mom," stuffed him with food and sent him home with bags of leftovers for his mother and sisters.

And now, looking down at Owen in his knit Ranger's hat and hand-me-down flannel jacket, Joe felt a swell of contentment.

"Ya think Van will like it?"

Joe hoped so. "She'll think it's dope."

"It kinda of takes up a lot of room."

"Yeah it does, and we'll probably have to cut off the top a little bit to get a star on it but that's okay. It really makes the place, don't you think?"

"Yeah." They both just stood looking up at the tree.

When Van had first suggested that the old stone building would convert into a perfect gift shop, Joe had thought she was being too optimistic. After all, they had just vatted their first very small crop of grapes. They had a long way to go.

But gradually she convinced the whole family that, in addition to wine and wine tastings, they could sell all things wine related: glasses, corkscrews, crackers, coolers, towels and other "go alongs." Joe had been skeptical.

Now he had to admit she was right. The building had survived several transformations, starting as an ice house, before being enlarged to a butter-churning room, then when the dairy closed, it became the storage for every piece of equipment, building material and general junk that the older Enthorpes refused to part with.

Van had dealt with them, too. Joe smiled, remembering. Who could hold out on a dynamo with a spreadsheet and business plan over a bottle of organic California wine that was made from grapes similar to the ones the Enthorpes grew.

So they'd cleaned out the building, carted all the crap to the dump, gutted the inside down to the studs and stone walls. They'd scrubbed and scraped, mopped and dusted, repaired and painted. The rudimentary kitchen and WCs used by the former farm hands had been refitted and spruced up.

That's as far as they'd gotten before they decided to hold the party there in its current state. Now the only thing in the room besides Joe and Owen was a twelve-foot spruce tree that took up one whole corner.

"It needs decorations," Owen said.

"Not tonight. It's time for you to get home."

"Aw, Joe, not yet. At least some lights. You don't want Van to come in and just see a plain old tree."

"I thought this was a great tree."

"It is but it'll be greater with some lights. It'll only take a few minutes."

Joe knew it would take more than a few minutes, but he didn't have the heart to disappoint the kid.

"You're getting all your homework done, right?" Joe asked.

"Yeah."

"That doesn't sound too enthusiastic."

"I know you said I oughta get an education, but it's so boring. I'd rather be working out here with you."

"You are working out here."

"I know, but all the time."

"What about hanging with your friends?"

Owen shrugged. "Have to come home and watch the girls til Mom gets home from work."

Joe nodded. He felt for the kid—living in an apartment in town with no free time to himself couldn't be easy. Joe had grown up in a large farm family. They'd all worked the dairy farm, but there was still time to do homework and have fun. His mom made sure of it.

"Okay, let's go look in those boxes Van ordered." Joe slit opened the cardboard carton that said Xmas Lights. Handed out a box to Owen, and another, and . . . There were ten boxes in all.

The two of them looked at each other.

"She probably doesn't mean to put all of these on the tree. Let's put some on and if she wants more we can add more."

"Good idea," Owen said.

Joe pulled the ladder over, detached the lights from their plastic frame. "You start getting the others out while I do the top, then it becomes a two-man affair."

It was a good half hour before they plugged in the lights.

Joe winced, there were big gaps of darkness and sections of overkill. Not the most skilled job he'd ever seen.

But when he glanced at Owen's face and saw the awe and sense of satisfaction there. He decided it was perfectly fine. Van would tweak it into beauty.

"All right. Time to close up here. I think we deserve a little snack before knocking off for the day."

With a final look at the tree, they turned out the lights and made their way across the yard to the house.

As he and Owen stepped into the enclosed back porch, they were surrounded by the aroma of freshly baked . . .

"Muffins," Owen said.

"Muffins," Joe agreed.

"You boys clean up before you track mud into my kitchen," Mom Enthorpe called from the kitchen. "I just mopped today."

Joe and Owen pulled off their hats and gloves and hung their jackets on pegs that stuck out along the back wall. A quick wash in the utility sink and they went inside.

Two tins of muffins sat on cooling racks on the counter.

"Those smell good," Owen said, and Joe's stomach rumbled.

"Well sit down and I'll get you a couple. Joe, get down the honey and butter.

"How about some milk or hot apple cider?"

"Cider," Owen said.

"Me, too," Joe said. He got the plastic jug of cider from the fridge and carried it to the stove.

"How's it going out there?" His mother asked as she heated the cider.

"The cleanup is done; the tree is up."

"With lights," Owen added.

"Excellent." His mother handed them mugs of steaming cider, poured herself a cup of coffee and sat down.

"Do I smell muffins?" Joe's grandfather stuck his head in the doorway, peered at Owen. "Who's that young man at our table?" he said.

It was ritual they went through every Saturday.

"It's me, Granddad Joe." Owen was already grinning.

"Lord, I hardly recognized you. You musta grown an inch."

Owen rolled his eyes. "One day you're gonna say that and I'm gonna be an inch taller."

"'Spect you will. Maybe next week." Joe Sr. snagged a muffin and sat down at the table. Mom Enthorpe slid a napkin under it as he put it on the tablecloth.

"Van's home," Joe Sr. said just as Joe heard a car come up the drive and stop by the side door.

"How did you know she was coming?" Owen asked. "I didn't hear anything."

"Ears like a fox," Joe Sr. said.

"And a nose like Pinocchio," added Joe's mother. "He saw the car through the window."

Joe pushed his chair back and went to meet Van. He stopped her at the back door.

"Hey," she said. She started to slip past him, but he grabbed her and kissed her. He knew she still felt uncomfortable when he showed affection in front of his family. After a childhood with fighting parents and an adulthood of self-protection, she'd come a long way, largely due to her acceptance by the Enthorpes.

"What are you lovebirds doing out there?" Granddad called.

"The laundry," Joe called back. And kissed her again.

There was plenty of room in the sprawling farmhouse. They hardly ever saw Matt, who was the only sib still in high school. Even with Elizabeth and Dave back from college for the holidays, they had plenty of privacy.

Still, he'd been working on a plan, one he hoped to be able to announce at Christmas. He wasn't sure how his family would react—or Van for that matter.

"What?" Van asked.

Joe shook his head. "Not a thing in the world."

Van slipped out of his arms and went into the kitchen, stopped to kiss his mother and then his grand-dad on the cheek. She made slurpy noises at Owen, who made a face and shied away in mock disgust.

Joe didn't get why Van didn't think she would be good with kids. Owen liked her just fine.

"Joe, it's almost five o'clock," his mother said.

"Right, I'd better get you home, Owen, or your mother will think we got lost. You want to come?" he asked Van.

"Sure." She'd just sat down but she stood back up.

"Give the girl a chance to catch her breathe," said Joe Sr. "She'll be here when you get back."

"I don't mind," Van said.

"No, Granddad's right," Joe said. "I'll see you in a few."

She sat down again.

His mother packed up food for Owen's mother and sisters and walked Joe and Owen to the door.

"See you next week, Owen."

He nodded. "Thanks for the muffins, Mom. And for . . ." He nodded toward the bag of food Joe was holding.

"You're welcome, sweetheart."

Once they'd both climbed into Joe's truck, Joe carefully placed the bag of food on the floor at Owen's feet. "She calls everybody sweetheart."

"I don't mind," Owen said. "But Van didn't see the tree."

"Oh." Joe had forgotten about the tree. "We'll let her discover it as a surprise. I'll tell her elves must have done it."

Owen rolled his eyes. "Like she's gonna believe that." He leaned back to look out the window.

Owen always got quiet when Joe drove him home. Joe didn't exactly get why, whether it was just winding down from the craziness of work and life at the winery or the prospect of going home to the duplex.

Joe had been inside. It was nice enough, better than most of the houses on their street, but it only had two small bedrooms. It had to be cramped for three growing children and especially hard for Owen in a house full of females.

Joe couldn't imagine what mornings must be like, or any other time. He'd grown up with six siblings, two parents, plus his grandfather after his grandmother had died. But there had been plenty of space and several bathrooms. A huge yard and outbuildings and acre after acre of pasture land.

Now Joe had more space than ever, yet he was anxious to get his own place with Van.

He sped up, itching to return home to Van and to his dinner, and a few minutes later, he turned onto the street where Owen lived.

He knew immediately that he wouldn't be home anytime soon. An ambulance with blinking lights was parked outside the duplex. The door to Owen's apartment was open wide. Something was terribly wrong.

Owen's younger sisters, Kayla and Haley, were standing in the yard clinging to a woman Joe didn't recognize.

He pulled the truck to the opposite curb just as EMTs rolled a stretcher from the Davises' duplex.

"Stay here," he told Owen but Owen jumped out of the truck before it came to a full stop. He ran toward the stretcher. "Mom! Mom?"

Joe parked the truck and hurried after him.

"Mom? What's wrong with her? Mom?" Owen tried to reach his mother, but one of the EMTs pulled him away.

"You're in the way, son. Let us take care of your mom. Now there's a good boy."

Joe grabbed Owen and held him back. "Where are you taking her?" he asked.

"County General."

"We'll meet you there." To Joe's untrained eye, Kathy Davis didn't look good at all.

The EMTs rolled the gurney onto the lift, climbed in after it and the ambulance sped away.

Joe turned Owen to face him, gave him a little shake. "We're going to go to the hospital as soon as we see about the girls. Okay?"

Owen just stared after the ambulance.

"Okay?" Joe didn't wait for him to acquiesce, but pulled him over to where Kayla and Haley were crying and fighting to get away from the woman who was holding them tight. He went over to her.

"You must be Joe."

Joe had to fight not to step away from the pervasive cigarette smell. The woman reeked of it. "I am."

"I'm Janice Cobb. I live across the driveway there."

"What happened?"

"She's been coughing her guts out," the woman said. "I been telling her to go see a doctor, but she wouldn't miss work. The girls usually stay with me on Saturdays til she gets home from work." Janice shook her head. "I saw her car come in the driveway, but when she didn't come to get them, I got worried and went to check on her. Kathy opened the door and just collapsed. I got her back to the couch and called 911. She didn't want me to call but I had to—she was looking bad."

Owen was clenching Joe's arm. With Mrs. Cobb's last statement, he started tugging at him. "Please, Joe, we gotta go to the hospital. Please."

"We're going now. Mrs. Cobb, can you watch the girls until I can find out what's going on?"

"I can." She detached herself from Kayla and Haley and took him aside.

"I can keep the girls overnight, but I don't have room for all three of them. Not with four of my own. If Owen don't mind staying by himself, I'll try to keep a watch out for him. But County's gonna come take them kids if she has to stay over. It don't look good for none of them."

"Let me find out what's happening and I'll get back to you."

He knelt down before the girls. "I'm going to go see about your mom. Then Owen and I will come back and tell you how she is, okay?"

They didn't nod, just stood there with tear-streaked faces and ill-fitting winter jackets.

"Come on, slugger, let's go see about your mom."

He and Owen climbed back in the truck. Joe got out his cell and called as he backed out of his space. Told his mother what was happening and slipped the phone back in his pocket.

Something told him this Christmas with Van was about to get a whole lot more complicated.

## Chapter Three

JOE'S FATHER, JOE Jr., came into the kitchen where Van and Mrs. Enthorpe were setting the table and Joe Sr. was supervising from his seat at the head of the kitchen table.

"That was Joe on the phone. Mrs. Davis was taken to the hospital and he's taking Owen there to see if they can find out what is wrong and what her condition is. He said to go on and eat without him."

Mrs. Enthorpe looked at her husband. "Oh dear, I hope it isn't anything serious."

"Me, too. He said he'd call as soon as he knew, so let's eat."

Mrs. Enthorpe pursed her lips. Shook her head. "And at Christmas. Those poor children." She lifted a plate of pork chops from the warming oven and put it on the table.

They all sat down and Joe Jr. said grace as he always did, only tonight he added the Davis family at the end. The prayer ended with everyone saying *amen*, including Van who had never once said grace as a child. She could barely remember eating a meal with her parents. Even when she'd been a teenager, the Enthorpes were the only real family she'd had. And that had blown up in her face.

She was slowly getting used to being in a family, but Van had been on her own completely since she'd run away all those years before, and it was hard for her just to relax and not wait for the other shoe to drop—for her to screw up again. It was hard for her to accept this kind of happiness.

Dinner was more subdued than usual. It had been a long week of working double duty for Van. And she'd been looking forward to spending a quiet night at home with Joe—as quiet as the Enthorpe home ever got.

And she was anxious to hear from Joe. She knew the Davises lived on the edge, one paycheck away from losing everything. Van remembered those days. She knew how hard they could be and she hadn't even had a family to support.

She never would. Not children anyway. Her cross to bear, and Joe's if she married him. She was glad he had Owen but it also made her acutely aware of her own failings. She'd told him to find someone else, someone who could give him children, and yet she stayed.

Was she being selfish? Should she just make the right decision for both of them?

She nearly jumped out of her chair when her cell phone rang.

"It's Joe," she said. "Excuse me."

She started to get up, but Joe Sr. said, "Answer it. We all want to hear."

"Hello?"

"Hey." Joe sounded tired.

"How is Mrs. Davis?"

"They're checking her in. They want to run some tests."

"Is she okay?"

"Um, they'll know more tomorrow. I may be here awhile longer."

"Where's Owen?"

"He's here." Joe lowered his voice. "He's worried."

Van lowered hers, not knowing if Owen was in listening range. "Is there real cause for alarm?"

"I'm not sure. The girls are at a neighbor's. He wants to spend the night at the hospital, but I'm going to bring him back to the farm, if that's okay."

"I'm sure it will be." Van looked to the others. "Joe wants to bring Owen home with him."

"Of course," Mom Enthorpe said. "Let me talk to him."

Van handed her the phone.

"Of course bring him here. And what about the girls?" She listened, then handed the phone back to Van.

"I'll be back as soon as I can, but I'll have to go get Owen some clothes and check on his sisters."

"Take what time you need. We'll keep dinner warm."

Joe chuckled softly.

"What?"

"You're beginning to sound like a farm wife."

"I doubt it." She could see Joe Sr. roll his eyes.

"Love you," Joe said.

Van looked around the table. Swallowed. "Me, too. Bye." She hung up to find three people watching her. Mom Enthorpe with sympathetic amusement, Joe Jr. with smug complacency and Joe Sr. with exasperation.

"Really, girl. A man tells you he loves you and you say 'me, too'? That the best you can do?"

Van blushed. "I don't do well with an audience."

"Leave Van alone," Mom Enthorpe said. "Not everybody is a blatant show-off like some men I know."

"Like your husband, you mean." Joe Sr. laughed. "Lordy, Van, you wouldn't have believed this guy, courting the young Alice here. Used so much aftershave and hair grease, you could smell him coming . . . and going. No kidding."

"Dad," Joe Jr. pleaded. He winked at Van and smiled at his wife.

And Van's heart and stomach thudded in tandem. One with longing, the other with sheer panic. All her time as a teenager, the Enthorpes had been more her family than her own parents were. Everyone had expected her and Joe to marry, and she'd wrecked it all. One night of misunderstanding, one misstep taken at the depth of her humiliation had almost cost her her life . . . and had cost her the ability to ever have children. She'd run from Whisper Beach and hadn't returned—until this past summer.

How could she ever live up to the Enthorpe paradigm of family? How could she ever be truly a part of them?

"Well, I think I'll get one of the spare bedrooms set up for Owen," Mom said. "Boys, you're in charge of cleanup. Van you go get comfortable and relax. You've been working yourself to the bone, and it's Christmas."

"I think I'll go check out the progress on the gift shop," Van said.

"Need company?" Joe Sr. asked.

"You," said Mom Enthorpe, "are doing the dishes."

Joe Sr. winked at Van. "Gotta be fast to get past that one."

Joe Jr. tossed him a dish towel.

Mom Enthorpe slowed down as she passed Van. "I believe the boys left you a surprise."

Van frowned. "That sounds ominous."

"They're very proud of it. But it might not be up to your standards."

"I'm sure it will be great," Van said, hoping they hadn't done something god-awful like paint the old stone walls or sand down the authentic wood moldings or . . . she couldn't even begin to imagine.

Mom Enthorpe gave her an impulsive hug. "I know you'll love it."

"Me, too." And Van hurried out of the room.

She shrugged into her jacket and went out into the crisp night air. It was dark, with a few stars in the sky peeking out of the accumulating clouds and Van wondered if they would wake up to snow tomorrow. Already the ground was beginning to crunch beneath her shoes, her breath made little clouds in the air.

It was peaceful, solitary. Normally Van liked peaceful and solitary, but these days she'd rather enjoy her peace and quiet with Joe. She reached the gift shop, looked around. Nothing out here. She unlatched the door and went inside.

It was dark with only a hint of the heat Joe must have turned down earlier. She sniffed. Sniffed again. Was that the faint hint of pine? Not the odor of the cleaning products on the shelves at Elite Managers, but straight from nature.

She turned on the light. And stared in awe.

In the far corner of the room was a tree. With a capital *T*. A monster tree that took up the whole corner where she'd planned to put the buffet table.

And so tall that the top was bent into a right angle against the ceiling.

Van bit her lip. One side of a smile slipped out from between her teeth. Then the other. Then she laughed. It was the largest, most inappropriate, whacked-out Christmas tree she had ever seen.

Now if she could just figure out what the hell to do with it. The buffet table could go on the opposite wall if she moved the . . . and the . . .

She stepped closer and realized that they had already started decorating it. She searched from the end of a string of lights and plugged it in.

The tree lit up. Whacked-out was right. It was so obviously decorated with love, if not spatial accuracy, that she laughed out loud. A joyful, happy mess of celebration, and she wouldn't do a thing to change it.

She'd been happy all those years before, the last time she'd spent a Christmas with the Enthorpes. When she and Joe had thought they were meant to be. Before the end of high school—before she ruined both their lives. And now she was back on the cusp of happiness. A tenuous, fragile happiness.

And with that happiness came the all-too-familiar fear that it wouldn't last, and she prayed that she wouldn't do anything to ruin it again.

She turned out the lights and returned to the house. There was no message from Joe, but while she'd been gone, the two senior Joes had finished the dishes, brought down the decoration boxes from the attic and were sitting in front of the television, watching the evening news.

Mom was sitting on the couch, looking through her recipe file, pulling out cards and reading them before either returning them to the box or putting them aside for the cookie-making day, which Van remembered was tomorrow.

The whole room smelled of freshly cut tree, which stood in front of the picture window. The bell choir poinsettias had arrived the day before and two sat on either side of the hearth. Wrapped packages had begun to collect in one corner.

She stood, suddenly hesitant in the doorway.

"Come sit." Mom patted the place beside her. "Do you like peppermint?" She showed Van a card with a picture of red-and-white cookies. "I usually make these pinwheel cookies with vanilla and chocolate, but I'm thinking about trying something different."

"Make your cherry brownies," Granddad called from his recliner, the only piece of furniture that had survived Mrs. Enthorpe's recent redecoration.

"I don't know how he can hear us with the television blaring like that," Mom Enthorpe said. "Not to worry, I'll make plenty of those, too."

"Peppermint sounds good. So does chocolate." Van shrugged apologetically. "I haven't made too many cookies since I moved to Manhattan." Cookie baking had been the last thing on her mind as she struggled to survive and then thrive as her business took off.

"Maybe we'll do both," Mom said.

"And some of those wedding cookies," Granddad said, emphasizing *wedding*.

Van flinched.

"You mean snowdrops?" Mom riffled through her recipe box, pulled out a card. "They're a staple of the holidays. I always make them and I always find powdered sugar in corners for weeks after the New Year." She sighed. "I wonder what is keeping Joe? I hope things aren't too dire. What a terrible time to be sick."

"Want me to call him?" Joe Jr. asked.

"No. He'll call when he knows something. Or he'll just come home."

Joe Jr. turned off the television and they all sat in silence for a while.

"I'm so glad you're here, Van," Mom said. "With everyone spread to the winds, I was beginning to think it was going to be just me and the three Joes for the holidays."

"Don't forget Duffy," Granddad said.

Hearing his name, the old hound dog, who was sleeping by the fireplace, raised his head, yawned then went back to sleep.

"What's wrong with the three Joes?" her husband asked as he came over to start looking through the recipes. "None of those date things, this year. They get stuck in everybody's teeth."

"Yes, dear." Mom gave her husband an angelic smile.

Van knew without a doubt she'd be making those date things, whatever they were. Alice Enthorpe was calm and compassionate and only raised her voice to be heard over the din of the other Enthorpes, never in anger. Yet she ruled her household without question.

"Maybe we should start stringing the lights while we're waiting for Joe. Come on, Dad, make yourself useful."

"No rest for the wicked," said Joe Sr. and pushed himself out of his recliner.

"Hey, Van, what did you think of the tree out in the creamery?"

"Gorgeous," Van said.

"Thought you'd get a kick out of it," Granddad said.

He chuckled. "Joe said Owen had picked out an even bigger one." He laughed out loud. "Lordy, we were afraid we wouldn't be able to get it through the door. Any bigger and we'd have to build around it."

He reached into one of the cartons and pulled out a box of lights.

Mom glanced up. "You're sure you don't want to wait for Joe?"

Her husband wagged his finger at her. "Is this going to be one of those jokes about how many Joes it takes to put up a string of lights?"

"No, just how many it takes to fall off the ladder."

"I haven't fallen off a ladder since 2005," he quipped back.

"She hasn't let you go up a ladder since then," said his father.

They all laughed and Van stood. "I'll go up the ladder."

Joe Sr. elbowed his son. "Works every time. Here you go, Van. Put this end at the very tip-top so we can plug in the star."

She took the cord, Joe Jr. got out the ladder and Van carried the cord to the top. By the time they were finished, Van had strung six strands of colored lights, and the two Joes were wearing felt Christmas hats and were draped in pieces of last year's tinsel.

They were standing back admiring their handiwork when they heard Joe's truck pull into the drive.

"Joe's home," Joe Sr. said.

"Perfect timing, that boy," said Joe Jr.

A few minutes later, the door opened and Joe walked in. "Look who I brought home."

He stepped to the side to reveal Owen, a stuffed backpack hung over one shoulder. And two young girls. They both had long, lanky blond hair about the same color as Owen's and were wearing inexpensive puff jackets that couldn't possibly keep out the winter cold.

"This is Haley," Joe said, indicating the taller one. "And Kayla."

"I'm four," Kayla said.

Haley didn't say anything.

"They're going to stay with us for a day or two."

Mom Enthorpe jumped from her couch and went to greet them, arms outstretched and smiling, though Van didn't miss the look of question that she shot her son.

Joe Sr. and Joe Jr. stood where they were like a couple of Christmas elves.

The girls stared at them. Owen bit his lip.

"Okay, guys, this is my mom and my dad and my granddad. We're all named Joe. Except for my mom—she's called Mom." Joe grinned at his family.

The two Joes nodded, setting off the bells on the points of their hats.

Van smiled, Owen snorted, but the girls just stared.

"Well, come on in and let's get you settled," Mom said. "Are you hungry? Have you had dinner? Joe, help bring the girls' cases back to Maddy's room. I've put Owen in Drew's room." She took charge of the girls, one on each side, and chattered at them as they disappeared into the hallway.

"I'll get Owen settled. We're all starving." Joe and Owen went off down the hall.

"Well, come on, Dad," said Joe Jr. "I guess we better unpack the food we just packed up."

Van watched everyone leave.

They all knew what to do. She didn't. She could organize and streamline the lives of total strangers. But she couldn't seem to get a handle on her own. Would she ever get this family thing figured out?

## *Chapter Four*

"I DIDN'T THINK you would mind," Joe told his mom as she handed him towels and washcloths.

"Of course not."

"The neighbor offered to keep the girls but she didn't have room for Owen and he didn't want to leave them there alone. Frankly, I didn't either. So I just packed them all up and brought them all here. I should have called first."

"You had your hands full. How is their mother?"

Joe shrugged, looked down the hall and lowered his voice. "They're keeping her for tests. I don't think it looks good. The neighbor said she's been pretty sick. A really bad cough. Pneumonia maybe? Hopefully nothing worse."

His mother nodded. "Pneumonia can be bad enough. You did the right thing."

"I feel bad about Van."

"Van? Why on earth?"

"This is all so new for her. It was hard enough to talk her into living out here with us. It's her first Christmas in a long time. Probably since we were in high school. I wanted to make it special for her."

"It will be special. Have you ever known a Christmas not to be?"

"I guess not."

"Now no more worrying. One thing at a time."

He followed her back to the bedrooms, dropped off towels and toothbrushes, showed the kids the bathroom and then led them back to the kitchen.

He was glad to see Van, his dad and his granddad already had places set and food on the table. The microwave beeped as they came into the kitchen. Owen went right to his usual place. Motioned for his sisters to sit down, which they were reluctant to do until his mother pulled out a chair for the older one, Haley, who sat down. Kayla climbed up to the seat next to her sister.

"We may need the dictionary," his mother said.

His father went to get the unabridged volume that had served as a booster seat since Joe could remember.

As soon as the kids were served, Joe excused himself and pulled Van back into the living room.

"Go eat before it gets cold again," she said.

He loved her so much he was stupid with it. He'd always loved her. Known from the first they were meant to be together. And if he hadn't been so clueless and stubborn, they would have been together all these years.

Those might have been their children sitting around the kitchen table instead of displaced kids whose mother could barely feed them and was now too sick to work.

But he *had* been clueless and stubborn and he was determined not to make the same mistakes now that Van had returned. He'd wanted this quiet night of tree decorating. A perfect way to ease Van back into the notion of being here permanently.

Not here, in his parents' house, but nearby on Enthorpe property. Joe had his eye on his grandparents' old farmhouse, closed-up since Granddad had come to live with them. It needed a lot of work, but it would be perfect—eventually.

"Joe? Are you all right?"

Joe started. "Yes, I just wanted to see you." He pulled her close and held on.

"Is it bad?" she whispered.

"The doctors don't know."

"Those poor kids."

"You don't mind that I brought them back with me?"

"Mind, why should I?"

"Just that I thought we'd have this quiet evening at home decorating and just hanging out, then all this. I'm sorry."

Van pulled away and stared at him. "You think I'm that selfish?"

"What? No. I just didn't want to disappoint you."

She sighed, shook her head. "I'm not disappointed. You should do what you want. It's your house."

That little sliver of ice in her voice stabbed Joe's heart. *It's yours, too,* he wanted to say. But it wasn't. It wasn't *their house.* It had taken all his and his family's persuasion to get her to move in with them instead of staying in town with Dorie Lister like she had planned.

His dad and granddad had fixed up the back wing as a suite so they'd have some privacy. One bedroom and a sitting room.

Van had been surprised that the family hadn't questioned their sleeping arrangements. Which was ridiculous. In their eyes, Van was already a member of the family. Now if he could just convince Van.

He scooped her back into his arms and kissed her. At first she was a little stiff. But not for long. He kissed her until she kissed him back; kissed her until she finally pulled away, laughing.

"Okay, I get it. I overreacted. Sorry. Long day."

He reached for her again, but she slapped him away. "Go get some food before Owen eats it all."

She took his arm and they went back into the kitchen. His granddad rolled his eyes when they squeezed through the door together.

"I was just saying to Haley and Kayla," his mother said, "that I didn't know if there would be visiting hours tomorrow at the hospital, but that it was Christmas cookie-baking day and we'd make some especially for her that you could take by later."

"Sure," Joe said. He sat at the place setting next to her and pulled a chair closer for Van. She passed him a platter of pork chops. "Glad you left me some," Joe said. "Van was afraid Owen might eat them all before I got back."

Owen smiled back at him, not his regular grin, but a good facsimile. Joe was proud of the boy. After his initial panic, he'd stayed calm and let Joe deal with the hospital.

There had been a minor skirmish when Owen had insisted on staying at his own house with his sisters. He didn't want them to stay with the neighbor. "She smokes all day and all night. It's bad for them to be over there."

Joe agreed. So he had invited them all to come home with him.

He looked over the table, every place taken for the first time since the last holiday. This was the way it should be. Family.

"Dope tree by the way," Van said to Owen.

This time Owen's grin was real.

BY THE TIME they finished dinner, they decided it was too late to finish decorating the tree and to postpone it until tomorrow. Mom took the girls off to get ready for bed.

Van considered asking if she needed help, but that would have been ridiculous. Mom had raised six children. She didn't need anybody's help, let alone Van's. So she started clearing the plates instead.

Taking that as a cue that everyone else was free, Owen and the three Joes wandered out to see what was on television.

*The Great Escape.* Van didn't mind. When she'd first come to live with Joe she'd been petrified that she might break a plate or a favorite dish. Which was absurd. She organized entire households, rearranged china closets, handled the finest crystal. She filed important documents, planned anniversary parties, screened nannies and made home-decorating decisions.

People called on her for every minutia of their daily life while they concentrated on business or volunteering or whatever they did that kept them too busy to take care of the basics. She was in demand.

And now she was elbow deep in sudsy water, washing pots and pans on a New Jersey farm. And it felt good. She still sometimes had to stop herself from rearranging the craziness of the Enthorpe cupboards or changing the traffic flow of the enclosed porch. She was learning to love the erratic nature of life with the Enthorpes; it was busy, messy, spontaneous, but it was full of life and love.

Van snorted. If her friends could see her now. But they could. Her friends were here. When she'd arrived in Whisper Beach a few short months ago, she was on her way to a posh vacation in Rehoboth. She hadn't meant to stay, hadn't wanted to say. Her past held some pretty unpleasant memories, but also some good. And the good won out.

Now she was commuting between Manhattan and Whisper Beach while she set up her second location. And then?

Really, was that a question? Why set up a location in Whisper Beach if you weren't planning to stay?

THE HOUSE WAS quiet and Van couldn't sleep. Maybe it was the prospect of opening two new businesses. Maybe it was the excitement of Christmas. The addition of three children to their midst. Her growing love for Joe and the equally growing indecision of whether she should could commit to life with him when she knew they might not work out. Despite what Suze said, she knew she could never divorce Joe, no more than she could turn her back on his family. Was she being selfish?

Just watching him tonight with Owen and his sisters made her realize how ill-equipped she was for being in this family. She didn't know how to do family, how to do kids, and she'd never know because she couldn't have them. And she knew Joe wanted children more than anything.

She turned slightly, watched his back rise and fall with sleep. Studied the moonlight glancing off his dark hair. She wanted to grab hold of him and all the Enthorpes and beg them not to let her go. At the same time she wanted to run until . . . until what?

She'd run once before. It had worked out in the end, but there had been some scary, awful times. She didn't want to be like that. She didn't want to lose her father again after just getting to know him. She'd never known him before. The father of her childhood had been a nasty drunk. Now he was the man he was supposed to be, should have been: sober, an artist, a compassionate human being. A father who loved her and whom she could love.

What on earth was she supposed to do?

She turned over, away from the window and the moonlight and away from Joe. She heard a sound, held still, and listened.

An animal call?

She sat up. It was coming from inside the house. One of the kids.

She slipped out of bed, hurried to the bedroom door and opened it a crack. She could hear crying coming from down the hall. She recognized that sound. Recognized and relived it as she stood in the doorway, indecisive, waiting for the whimpering to turn to full-fledged terror.

"What are you doing?"

Van whirled around. Joe was propped up on one elbow and squinting at her.

"One of the kids is crying," she said.

"Oh." He pushed the covers back, grabbed his jeans off the back of the chair and grabbed his tee-shirt as he headed for the door. "Go back to sleep. I'll take care of it." He brushed past Van and met his mother coming down the hall in the opposite direction.

How had she managed to hear the crying from the other side of the house?

Joe and his mother didn't have to exchange words, they simply opened the door to the girls' bedroom just as a scream erupted from the room.

Van grasped the doorjamb, her own remembered terror holding her there.

Joe and his mother went inside, shutting the door behind them. The screaming finally tapered down to exhausted sobs.

Van turned from the door and got back into bed, pulled the covers up to her chin, her knees to her chest, and lay there shaking. From cold, she told herself. But she knew it was really from inside, the cold dread of memory that still overtook her even in the best of times.

The nights when her father was drunk and angry, the terror of living with strangers in Manhattan, other runaways and immigrants who worked for the cleaning service where she'd found work. The terror of knowing she was going to die when she began to lose the baby she'd made with a stranger because she'd been so betrayed by Joe and life.

Oh, she recognized the terror in that little girl. She'd wanted to reach out to her, tell her she was safe here.

She'd wanted to comfort them, tell them that everything would be fine. But even if she'd gone instead of Joe and his mother, she couldn't have told them that. No one knew what would happen in their lives. They could only hope. Small comfort to a terrified child . . . or adult for that matter.

She couldn't even convince herself, so she'd let Joe go instead.

From down the hall, she heard a door open and shut, Joe and his mother talking in low tones as they walked back down the hall. And as selfish as it was, Van felt her own shortcomings more than ever.

And when the bedroom door opened, and Joe came back to bed, Van pretended to be asleep.

## Chapter Five

IT WAS ALMOST nine when Van awoke the next morning. It had taken a long time for her to fall asleep after the crying in the night. And then she'd slept like the dead. She didn't hear Joe leave, but when she got out of the shower, she heard voices from the kitchen.

She meant to get a cup of coffee and take it out to the gift shop to do some work. When she looked into the kitchen, Haley and Kayla were sitting at the table. Mom was at the sink drying dishes.

"Morning," Mom said. "There's a plate of pancakes warming in the oven for you."

"Sorry, I overslept."

"Did you have plans for today?"

"Just . . . working on the gift shop." Van poured a cup of coffee. "I finished stocking Elite yesterday. Now I just have to hire and train some staff and I'm ready to go."

"Then sit down and have a nice leisurely breakfast." Mom Enthorpe reached into the oven.

"Where are Joe and the guys?"

"I sent Joe and Owen to the store and the other two decided that they had to go along. They said they had a few things to do. I'd like to think they're getting haircuts, but since it's Sunday, I know the barber isn't open. Maybe last-minute Christmas shopping."

She placed a plate of pancakes in front of Van, followed by butter and syrup.

"These look delicious."

"Well enjoy, and if you can spare the time, we're making Christmas cookies this morning. We could use another pair of 'big' hands."

*Cookies?* "I . . ."

"We're so excited, aren't we, girls?"

"I don't know much about making cookies." Cookies were about as far out of her résumé as they could be.

"We don't either," Kayla said. "But it's fun." She smiled.

And Van thought, *She has such tiny teeth.*

Haley nodded but didn't add her opinion.

Van studied both girls, trying to discern which one had been so upset during the night. She couldn't tell since they were both a little puffy from sleep. Their hair had been combed. By Mom Enthorpe? Or had they already learned to take care of themselves? Joe said their mother worked two jobs. What on earth would they do if she was incapacitated for any length of time?

Mom was smiling at her and Van realized the two

girls were looking at her, too. They were all waiting for a response.

"I bet it's fun."

"Good. The more the merrier." Mom handed Van an apron. "It could get messy."

*Messy.* Van tied the apron around her waist and spread it over her lap. Van hated messy. A few months ago, she would have already reorganized the kitchen, refolded the dish towels and rearranged the shelves in the pantry. She'd recently revamped Dorie's whole restaurant.

Over the summer, she'd gotten used to Suze, the quintessential absentminded professor, spilling food down her front. At Dorie's, she'd stopped rearranging toiletries in the shared bathroom.

Then she'd moved in with the Enthorpes who could leave tornado devastation in their wake. It hadn't been easy at first, but she found herself not cringing when a newspaper fell off the chair arm onto the floor. Or bags of groceries sat on the table for hours. Of course, she'd learned that Mom had her own system, and that all the unpacked bags contained nonperishables that she could unpack at her leisure.

*But cookies?* Cookies were what housewives made. Mothers. Grandmothers. Where did that leave Van? Here in the Enthorpe's kitchen where food and eating was not just a necessary habit but a communal sharing. It was hard to get used to at first. As the only child of a drunk and nurse who worked odd hours, she'd never known familial togetherness, or much about sharing.

She poured more syrup on her pancakes. "Great, cookies." Everybody could make cookies. You just followed the recipe.

She'd made cookies before. Nobody grew to be thirty without ever making cookies. The memory came with her last bite of pancake. She'd made cookies, or at least helped, in this very kitchen. Maddy and Elizabeth and Mom and her.

They'd worn aprons and laughed and eaten the cookie dough until Mom ordered them to stop. She could barely swallow her food as the memory invaded her. Happy times, happy times again, if she let them be.

Mom Enthorpe cleared the girls' plates; outfitted them in aprons that she had to roll up several times to keep the kids from tripping on them; got out bowls, utensils, flour, sugar, eggs, butter, cans and boxes until Van and her plate were a little oasis of sanity in a sea of . . . She gulped. Chaos.

Van got up and carried her plate to the sink, washed it and put it away.

"Ready," she said. "Where do we start?"

"We're starting with sugar cookies," Mom said.

"We're going to decorate them," Kayla volunteered.

Haley hadn't said anything since Van had joined them. Was she upset? Or shy? Or angry? Maybe Van was just reading her own experience into Haley's expression, but she didn't think so.

Mom and Kayla measured and poured, and Haley and Van mixed the ingredients together. By the time the first batch of Christmas-tree-and Santa-shaped cookies were put in the oven, the table, the floor, the chairs and the bakers were covered in flour.

"Should we do a little cleanup?" Van asked, running her hands under the spigot.

"Heavens no," Mom said. "We're just getting started."

JOE AND OWEN sat in the backseat of the farm truck. His father was driving and Granddad was riding shotgun. They were on their way to the original Enthorpe farmhouse, down the road a half mile from the current house.

Thank God his granddad had refused to let them sell the house when they'd had to sell off acreage several years before. Joe loved the old house, everyone did. Even though now they were all too busy to do more than basic maintenance.

Joe had never really broached the idea of him and Van moving into the old house. He didn't know what his granddad's reaction would be. He'd lived with his wife and children in that house for over fifty years. He might not want anyone else to live in it.

He hadn't even mentioned the possibility to Van.

Her Manhattan apartment was sleek—to Joe's mind, downright cold—and he wasn't sure that the farmhouse would hold any appeal for her.

Maybe it was a stupid idea. But this morning when his granddad suggested they take a ride over and see "what was what" after the last storm, Joe thought maybe today was the day. So right after breakfast, they'd all piled into the truck.

The house stood behind a copse of trees, the branches barren now, and Joe could just catch glimpses of it as they turned into the drive. He leaned forward to see through the front windshield.

*Funny, how the memory plays tricks on you*, he thought. In his mind's eye he saw white clapboard and dark green shutters. At Christmas the eaves over the porch would be draped with pine boughs and white lights. The fir tree in the yard would be covered with red bows and suet balls for the birds. Like his parents' house was now.

So it was a shock to see it looking untended and uncared for. One of the shutters on an upstairs window had pulled off its hinges. The whole house needed painting. In the ten years his grandmother had been gone, the house had aged a hundred.

His father stopped the truck at the front of the house and they all got out.

"When did that happen?" his granddad asked, pointing up to the hanging shutter.

"Probably in that big storm we had a few weeks ago," Joe Jr. said. "I should've come over and made sure everything was okay."

"Naw. You and Joe have been busy with the vineyard. I shoulda come before now. Should keep a better eye on things."

They all looked up at the house, and Joe saw his opening.

"Since we're here," he said. "There's something I've been thinking about."

Both Joes—and Owen—turned to look at him.

"What's that?" Granddad asked. "You're not thinking of razing the place to put in more vines." It was a statement not a question, and the way his granddad's chin was jutting said if that's what Joe was thinking he could just think again.

"No. Nothing like that. I was just thinking ahead, you know of the future . . ." He swallowed. He should have discussed this with his father before even broaching the subject, but suddenly with Christmas coming on and the children in the house and Van and him living together in all the hoopla. . . .

"I was going to ask you what you thought about maybe if Van and I moved in here. We could fix the place up—not changing anything or anything." God he was tongue-tied.

"You asked that girl to marry you yet?" his granddad asked.

"Not exactly."

His father and grandfather exchanged looks. Then like two mechanical toys, they turned their heads simultaneously to look at Joe.

"It's complicated," Joe said.

"No it isn't." His grandfather shook his head, exasperated. "Only takes four little words. *Will you marry me?* Count 'em."

Owen's eyes had rounded, now his mouth followed suit.

"I'm not sure she'll say yes."

"Hell, she's living with you under our roof. That's as near to married as you can get without the preacher pronouncing it."

"That was hard enough."

"You using the house as incentive to seal the deal?"

"No," Joe said. He wasn't. He just thought if they could be truly alone, have their own place to start building a family, or maybe not a family, but spending the rest of their lives together.

"It was just a thought," Joe said.

"Well, we'd best go take a look and see what needs to be done."

Joe had already turned to go back to the truck, but his granddad's sentence made him stop.

"Come on then." Joe Sr. started toward the house. Joe's dad put his hand on Joe's shoulder and gave him a short nod.

"Wow," Owen said and hurried after Joe Sr.

Joe and his father followed.

By the time his granddad had unlocked the door, Joe's heart was hammering. He hoped he wasn't jumping the gun on this. What if Van said no? To the house and to him?

Owen slipped past Granddad and went inside and the three Joes followed after. It was cold inside. For several years after his grandmother died, they'd kept the utilities paid up, but gradually they'd drained the pipes and let the electricity and heat go.

The four of them stood in the archway, looking into the "parlor" as it had been called when Joe was a boy. Most of the furniture had been claimed by those who wanted it or been carted off to the Vets. A few pieces were still sitting in awkward disarrangement in the abandoned rooms. Two armchairs faced the fireplace, probably the home of mice now.

What his father or grandfather was thinking, Joe couldn't begin to guess. Were they reliving the good old days? He knew he was. Imagining the Christmas tree twice as large as the one they had at the farmhouse. The ceilings here were a good twelve feet high. Those had been incredible days, when Great Uncle Jessup had played Santa and none of the kids, at least not Joe, ever guessed he wasn't.

By tacit agreement, no one had ratted him out, teased the younger kids about him not really being Santa. Until they day he died, no one had ever breathed a word that the real Santa had never appeared. To them Uncle Jess was the real deal.

And Joe wanted that. His brothers and sisters were moving away. They still mostly made it back for holidays, but soon they'd have their own families and would be too busy to keep the family tradition alive.

They would make their own traditions in their new homes in their new towns. And he would make his, hopefully with Van, and with their children, even if those children were adopted. Would it be enough for him? For her?

They moved on to the kitchen, another large farmhouse room. The wallpaper was faded and curling along the seams in places, but the heavy wooden oak table that no one had room for still stood in the center of the room.

Joe placed his palms on the surface, pushed it back and forth to see if it wobbled. But it was steady as a rock.

The appliances had been removed, but they would have to be replaced anyway. Was he totally off the mark to think that Van would even want to live here?

"Are you sure Van wouldn't rather live in a one of those nice modern condos down the road?" asked his father, reading his thoughts.

Joe shrugged. He didn't really know what Van wanted. He wasn't sure that Van knew what she wanted. But they couldn't muddle around not knowing forever. It was time to take a stand. Maybe.

They left the kitchen and moved to the back of the house where a more modern bathroom had been installed when his grandparents had moved downstairs.

The dining room had been converted into a spacious bedroom. It would do as a master suite until they could tackle the upstairs.

There were four more bedrooms and a bath upstairs. And another two overflow rooms in the attic above.

"It's a lot of house," said Joe's father.

"Take a lot of work," added his granddad.

"I thought we could just fix up the downstairs first, then do the upstairs later. As time went on."

"For kids," Owen said. "I would so live here."

Joe's breath stuttered. He was aware of his father and grandfather preternaturally quiet beside him.

"I mean . . . some other kid. Your kids."

"We know what you mean," Granddad said. "And if Joe fixes up the place you and your sister and momma will have to come visit."

Owen frowned. "Yeah."

For one selfish moment, Joe had agreed with him. But Owen had a family who loved him. And hopefully his mother would get well soon and could find a better paying job. Maybe they'd even find something here at the winery for her. He'd have to ask Van.

It wasn't really Owen's future he was worried about. It was his and Van's.

"Well, we'd better get going before Alice thinks we've absconded with the condensed milk and slivered almonds." His father herded Owen downstairs.

"Get Ollie Leesom to come over and inspect the structure and wiring," Granddad said. He took a final look around. "It would be nice to have someone in the house again. It would be nice to have you and Van."

Joe followed him downstairs. He'd seen the mist in his granddad's eyes and he was feeling a little teary himself.

They all climbed back into the truck.

"Don't mention this to Van," Joe told them. "I want it to be a surprise."

"No problem, son, none of us will breathe a word."

"Not even you, Owen."

"I won't. But I don't see what the big deal is. It's a great house."

It was a great house, Joe thought as they backed out of the drive. A great, big house. Big enough for a huge family, like Granddad's and like his own parents'. But would it be too big for Joe and Van alone?

## Chapter Six

VAN HAD NEVER seen so much flour, sugar, sprinkles and frosting in her life, and it seemed to her they were wearing most of it.

She was surrounded by bowls and racks and cookie sheets. Every counter was crowded with cookies in various states of completion. Across the hall the dining room table had been cleared to accommodate the colorful Christmas tins that would eventually be filled with an assortment of the seemingly endless variety of cookies, bars and clusters.

Van reached for the white piping. She was beginning to get the knack of outlining the lemon star cookies. Her first attempts looked more like Kayla's than those of a proficient adult. Haley was the real pro. She'd perfected getting a straight line of frosting along the edges almost immediately, then she branched out to adding clusters of sprinkles and finishing each point with a silver dragée.

Van finished her outline with only a little blob and a few squiggles and glanced over to Haley, who was sitting next to her. The girl had added a face to her latest cookie, a face with flowing yellow hair and big blue star eyes made from edible confetti.

"Wow," Van said.

Haley shrugged.

"I used to make paintings on sea shells and sold them in the five-and-dime," Van said.

"You didn't."

"I did. So I can tell you that cookie looks pretty professional to me."

Haley's eyebrows lifted a minutely. "It does?"

Van nodded, then turned hers around for Haley to see.

Haley's mouth twitched, then she hiccupped and a little laugh escaped.

"I know, pretty awful."

"You just need practice," Haley pronounced and went back to her cookie.

As far as conversations went, Van wouldn't call it fascinating, but it was the most the girl had spoken to her all morning and they'd been sitting elbow to elbow for a couple of hours.

She tried again. "Do you make a lot of cookies?"

"No. We did when my grandma lived with us."

Van nodded, wondering if her grandmother was dead and whether she should ask.

She cast a glance at Mom Enthorpe but she was busy on the other side of the room.

Should she interfere? Had Joe already contacted the grandmother to let her know that her daughter was in the hospital? What if she didn't care? What if she was dead and mentioning her might upset the children more than they already were?

"But that was a long time ago."

"I see. When you were Kayla's age?"

"Not that long, last year." Haley sighed. "When she left we stopped doing a lot of things. Mom doesn't have the time. We don't have the money. In case you haven't noticed."

Whew. Hit a nerve.

"We had more money when grandma was there."

"Did she die?"

Haley's head snapped toward her. "No, she had a fight with Mom and left."

"Oh. Does she know your mom is in the hospital?"

Haley shrugged.

"Does she live around here?"

"No."

Haley pushed her chair back and carried her finished cookie over to the counter.

When she sat back down and reached for another cookie to decorate, she turned away from Van. It was pretty clear Van's attempt at conversation was over.

Kayla on the other hand, chatted nonstop from where she was perched on her knees on a chair at the head of the table. She seemed to be wearing as much cookie dough as there was on the counter in front of her. There was a glob of green icing stuck in her hair.

Van squelched a shudder. Who knew kids could be so messy? The children of her clients were always clean and immaculately dressed. She assumed that was the work of the nanny, though several clients gave Van credit for organizing their lives so that the craziness was kept under control.

"Look, Haley!" Kayla pushed a ball of red dough onto her nose.

Van made a note to dispose of it before it made its way back into the bowl.

"I'm Rudolph. Rudolph, the red nosed reindeer . . ." She began to sing in a loud monotone.

"Had a very shiny . . ." Mom added her smooth soprano voice to Kayla's. And soon they were all singing about Rudolph. Van didn't think she'd remember the words, but surprisingly she did. Even Haley deigned to mumble along, every now and then allowing a word to sound in its entirety.

They set the stars aside to dry. Moved onto "Frosty the Snowman" while they dropped chocolate chip cookies onto freshly greased baking sheets.

They were halfway through "We Wish You a Merry Christmas" when the back door opened, bringing in a frigid gust of air and the guys.

"Man, it smells great in here," Owen said, shrugging out of his jacket.

Granddad headed straight to the counter. "Lemon stars," he said, pulling off his gloves.

"One." Mom held up one finger in case the verbal directive had passed him by.

"And all four of you get back into the mudroom and take off your coats and hats. And make sure your gloves make it to the basket and don't wind up on the floor."

The three Joes and Owen backed out of the kitchen. The sounds of scuffling ensued.

Mom shook her head. "Put home-baked cookies in front of grown men and they act no older than Kayla here."

Kayla smiled a broad smile that showed her crooked little primary teeth, now tinged with blue from icing she'd been licking.

When the guys came back in, Mom pointed to the far corner of the counter. "You can have those broken ones. And don't spoil your dinner."

"We haven't had our lunch," her husband informed her.

She looked up at the kitchen clock. An old round wall clock that Van remembered had been there when she was a girl. "Good heavens, I just lost track of time. Come on, girls. We'd better call it a day and clean up. We still have a tree to decorate."

"Christmas tree," Kayla squealed and clapped her hands.

Haley didn't comment, just bent over another cookie she was decorating with a moon and star.

Van stood, dislodging flour and bits of dough from her lap.

She looked up to see Joe and his granddad looking at her.

"What?"

Joe's smile turned to a grin.

"What?"

The grin turned to a laugh. "Come on." He took her by the shoulders, turned her around and marched her out of the kitchen and down the hall to the powder room. Held her while he turned on the light then nudged her toward the mirror.

Van gaped at the image reflected back to her. There was flour in her two-hundred-dollar take-no-prisoners haircut. A series of icing dots and dashes created a colorful holiday Morse code across her cheeks and forehead.

She shook her head minutely, became aware of the Joes and Owen, and the two girls and Mom Enthorpe crowded into the bathroom doorway.

"I don't think I've ever seen you so festive," said Granddad. "It's a good look on you."

Van looked back over her shoulder and rolled her eyes at him.

"I mean it."

"It was Owen's fault," she said.

"Me? I wasn't even here."

Van laughed. She couldn't help herself. Then they were all laughing. Everyone but Haley.

"Good grief," Mom Enthorpe said when they'd finally backed away from the door. "We were having such a good time, I forgot to put the lasagna in the oven."

"Lasagna?" Owen asked.

"We always have lasagna at Christmas," Joe said.

"Then go get it out of the back fridge while I clean up the kitchen."

Joe and Owen went off to retrieve the lasagna while Joe Jr. and Joe Sr. looked on in amusement.

"I'll help clean up." She brushed past them and hurried back to the kitchen.

It was a disaster area. She took a deep breath. She knew how to deal with messes.

Mom Enthorpe was transferring trays of cookies into large plastic containers. "Another day or two and we should have enough sweets to pack up and deliver."

*Another two days?*

"Who are they going to?" Van asked as she carried two big containers out to the dining table.

"Friends, neighbors. We'll take some over to Drew and his crew, and there are several family members we don't really see much of during the year. And the girls at the post office and the hair salon and . . ."

The list went on. Van thought how much easier it was to send a fruit basket or stick a check in an envelope and call it Happy Holidays. And no cleanup time, she thought as she surveyed the mountains of dirty dishes and leftover cookie makings.

But not nearly as much fun.

She methodically set about cleaning up. Haley hung around the fringes of the room, doing a chore if she was told, but not taking the initiative. Kayla started carrying things she could reach to Mom who was rinsing bowls and loading the dishwasher. "It makes so much noise, but it will be finished by the time the lasagna is ready to eat."

*Small favors*, Van thought, thankfully.

Van sent Haley to the closet for a broom and dustpan. Then she sat Kayla down to clean the cookie dough off the bottom of her sneakers.

She was retying the girl's shoes when Joe came in. He stopped on his way to the stove, watched her without a word, then got a glass of water and left the room.

Van stood to find Mom watching her; she looked away. She had to stop reading meaning into every gesture or look. It had gotten worse since she'd moved in with the Enthorpes.

She'd been horrified at the prospect when Joe first suggested it. But Joe and Mom and Suze and Dorie had talked her into it. Now she loved living here, and she loved Joe. But still there was that little thing—big thing, really—about children. She just wished she knew what to do.

She and Joe had talked and talked and talked. But

she couldn't help looking down the road as the years went by and there were no children. Every time she saw him with Owen, she felt it down to her gut. Not jealousy, but a sense of not being enough. Ever.

It didn't take long to clear the kitchen. The lasagna was in the oven. Salad was made; the table was set. Everything in its place and on schedule for dinner like a well oiled-machine. Or an active well-used, well-loved kitchen.

Joe came in to tell them he had called the hospital. Mrs. Davis was doing better but visitors were still not allowed. The news cast a pall over the next few minutes until Granddad mentioned the Kennans' Labrador had just had puppies a couple of weeks before and they all piled into Mom's car to go check them out.

"Do not come home with any more dogs," Mom called after them, then turned to look at Van.

"See what you have to look forward to?"

And Van lost it. Without warning, without even knowing what she was feeling or that this simple sentence could unleash all her misgivings, Van burst into tears.

"Van, what's wrong?"

"Nothing. I just can't—Sorry, so stupid." Van rushed from the room.

She'd managed to pretty much pull herself together by the time she reached her and Joe's room. She felt like such a fool and was humiliated to lose it in front of Joe's mom, who would probably tell Joe and Joe would be all sympathetic and attentive and worried. None of them would get that she just wanted to be treated normally.

The pressure was more than she could bear sometimes. She should just leave and go back to the life she'd made for herself. She'd been happy then, happy enough—but not as happy as here with Joe and the Enthorpes.

There was a tap at the door.

She didn't want to talk to Mom. But she had to let her in or things would get blown totally out of proportion.

She got up from the side of the bed and opened the door.

Mom Enthorpe held up a bottle of wine and two glasses. "My bad. Brought us these. Sitting room?"

Van nodded and followed Mom back to the extra guest room that had been converted to a snug little den.

They sat down; Mom poured. They clinked glasses. Sipped. The wine was good. Not theirs, but from a French vineyard where Joe had apprenticed.

"We're all trying just too damn hard," Mom said.

Van blinked. She'd never heard Alice Enthorpe say anything worse than *shoot*.

"We love you so much, and want you to stay with us, that we're falling over our own feet and end up saying or doing stupid stuff to drive you away."

Van shook her head, but it was true.

"It was unthinking of me to say that."

"No," Van blurted out. "It's what it should be. It's what families expect and should be, and what I can't be."

Mom sipped, considered. She didn't rush in to deny it and Van's hope sank on the dim horizon.

"I guess that's what most people expect. That the younger generation should carry on the family name. That's a pretty lame excuse for marrying someone."

"Not if that's what you want."

"Ah."

Neither of them spoke for a while, then Mom put down her glass. She took Van's hand. "I can't speak for Joe, only he can. But I can tell you that you're my daughter just as sure as if you were born an Enthorpe. You have been since the day Joe first brought you to visit. And those three kids out there, they could be, if it comes to that. But I don't know what you think, what you feel—what you want. Do you?"

Van shrugged. "I did. Before. I thought I would marry Joe and we'd spend the rest of our lives together on the dairy farm."

Mom sighed a smile. "So did we."

"And that we'd have lots of children like we talked about. He told me I'd be a good mother, even though I didn't have a good home life. That when I was married to him I would know my real self and know that I could do anything."

"Just like a man. But you have to love them in spite of their rocks for brains sometimes."

"I know it seems silly and arrogant, but it kept me going all through high school and then after—after I screwed everything up and had to make a different life. It kept me going, him saying that I could do anything.

"But now I can't do the one thing that means the most to him."

"Huh." Mom poured a little more wine in both their glasses. "You're talking like it's the nineteenth century. If you want kids, there are thousands of children who need loving parents like you and Joe would be. I've told Joe that and I'll tell you. We don't need any more grandchildren to carry on the name of Enthorpe. God knows the Enthorpes litter the whole east coast. And if you don't want any kids at all. That's fine, too."

"I do. I just don't know how to . . ."

"You will."

"Will I? It seems like I take two steps forward and then everything gets screwy. How did you make it work?"

Mom laughed. "You're working with a basic flaw in your expectations."

"I don't know anything about kids."

"That's not it. You think life goes in a straight line. A to B, then if you do C, it goes to D? It doesn't."

"It would be better if it did."

"Maybe, but it's sloppy and zigzaggy and exasperating and wonderful—and sometimes painful. You just have to hang on for the ride."

"But you always kept things running smoothly."

"Ha. Most of the time it's like herding soap bubbles, or should I say snowflakes? Look out the window."

Van did. It was snowing. Flakes drifted past the window, so delicate that most of them would disintegrate when they landed.

"Now I'd better get back to the lasagna or we'll have some real unhappy folks. You stay and finish your wine, have a good cry if you need to."

Van shook her head. "Don't tell Joe. I'm fine. Really."

"You're more than fine, Vanessa Moran. And I'd be proud to have you as a daughter-in-law."

## Chapter Seven

VAN FINISHED HER wine, took a quick shower and looked for something festive to wear for the tree decorating. She came up with not much. Black jeans and a burgundy boat-neck sweater that she'd bought on a whim on one of her rare trips to the mall with Suze. She'd mentally filed the sweater under expanding-your-horizons, put it in the back of the closet and promptly forgot about it—until tonight.

She quickly put on makeup, checked that she hadn't missed any dabs of dough or food coloring in her quick ablutions and went down the hall to help with dinner.

She felt kind of stupid about her outburst earlier and wanted to apologize to Mom Enthorpe before the others returned, but she was too late. She ran headlong into the group coming through the front door.

Granddad took a look at her and whistled. Joe elbowed him in the ribs and came to give Van a kiss.

"It's snowing and we saw puppies," Kayla announced. "I got to hold them."

"Had to pry her away," said Joe, still holding Van.

"Good thinking. Christmas isn't exactly the easiest time to house train."

He laughed. "You are a wealth of information."

Van shrugged. "Part of the services. Now let me go help your mom get dinner on the table."

"You or lasagna? Hmmmm." Joe dropped his arms and opened his palms, pretending to weigh the options. "You . . . lasagna . . . you . . lasagna. You . . ."

"Lasagna!" their audience yelled.

Van punched him and went into the kitchen.

Dinner was consumed at lightning speed. It seemed even Mom Enthorpe was looking forward to decorating the tree. Van offered to do the dishes, but Mom nudged her out of the kitchen and into the living room where Christmas music was playing from the CD player and Granddad was handing out ornaments.

"It's going to be a free for all," Van said.

"Always is," Mom said, handing her a paper-wrapped ornament.

Van slowly unwrapped it to reveal a green-and-red glass hummingbird.

"We bought that at a gift shop in North Carolina. We'd taken the children there for a vacation and there were hummingbird feeders all along the windows of the dining room. Every morning the feeders were three deep in hummingbirds. They were so industrious, so beautiful."

Van carefully carried the ornament to the tree, avoiding Granddad and Owen, who were nudging each other for the same branch. Van looked for a safe place to hang the delicate bird and keeper of so many memories. A safe place, but a place where everyone could see it. High up so no one would mistakenly hit it and knock it to the ground. She found an empty place, hooked the hummingbird over the branch and tested to make sure it wouldn't fall.

She turned to see Joe watching her. He smiled at her with such love it hurt her heart. She smiled back and turned away.

"Better shake it, Van," Granddad said, "before these rapscallions use up all the decorations."

The tree was filling up quickly, mostly the bottom half since that was as high as the girls could easily reach. While the two older Joes unwrapped garland, and Joe and Owen hung decorations from their ears, Mom Enthorpe sat on the sofa, legs up, viewing the proceedings with satisfaction.

Once every last decoration had found a place and golden glass beads had been draped around the tree, they all stood back to survey the scene.

As "Once in David's Royal City" began to play, Joe Jr. reached for his wife's hand. "And now for the pièce de rèsistance."

Mom took his hand and he pulled her up from the couch.

Granddad produced a ladder and Joe Jr. helped his wife climb until she could reach the top of the tree, then he handed her a star, brilliant and old. A star that Van was sure had seen many Enthorpe Christmases. She placed it at the very top of the tree, plugged it into the string of lights, made a few minor adjustments and climbed down again.

"Always save the best for last," said Joe Jr., and then he kissed his wife.

Joe plugged in the lights and everyone applauded. Van shivered. It was beautiful.

And amid those hundreds of little lights, the music and the star, Van realized that this was what family was, the traditions growing with each year until they became the fabric that held them together through the years, through the good stuff and the bad.

Van had never known that, only anger and despair. And she vowed in that moment never to let that happen to her own family—She stopped herself. She would never have that kind of a family.

The carol ended and Mom and Van began cleaning up the wrappings and returning them to the storage boxes.

"I want my mommy," Kayla cried suddenly and burst into tears.

Mom knelt down beside her. "I know you do, honey. And you'll see her in a day or two."

"I want her now."

Mom took her hand and led her over to Granddad's recliner. She sat down and pulled Kayla up beside her and held her while she cried. "Your momma's getting better at the hospital. And you'll be able to see her soon. But right now she has to be in the hospital to get well. And we want her to get well, don't we?"

Kayla nodded against Mom's shoulder.

"It will only be a little while, and then you'll all be back together again." Mom looked up to Joe.

He looked back.

"That's right, Kayla," Owen said. "Momma doesn't want you to cry. It would hurt her feelings when everybody's been so nice to us."

Kayla turned her head enough to look at him. "But I want to go home."

"I know. And we will. Soon."

Mom wrapped things up after that. It was early but she sent the girls off to get ready for bed. "I'll come check on you in a minute."

"I'm going to start putting these boxes back in the closet," Joe Jr. said.

Granddad had something he needed Owen to help him with back in the den, and Joe, Van and Mom were left in the living room.

"We haven't had a chance to talk," Mom said. "How serious is her condition?"

Joe shrugged. "They still doing tests, but they couldn't speak with me since I wasn't a relative."

"Do they have a father?"

"No one seems to know. And Mrs. Davis was too far out of it to say anything."

"But you checked her in?"

"No. She had her Medicaid card in her purse. The police asked me some questions, but one of them knew me from Mike's Bar, a friend of Jerry Corso. I told him I'd take care of the kids. He called Jerry, who vouched for me. I signed a form and that was it. I'm guessing if Kathy Davis is not able to okay us to keep them, the county will send around a social worker at some point."

Van shuddered.

"There are no other relatives?" Mom Enthorpe asked.

"I don't know."

"A grandmother," Van said. "Haley said their grandmother used to live with them, but she and the mother had a fight and she moved out."

"Did she say where she was?"

"I don't think she knew. Maybe Owen would."

Joe called to Owen, who came down the hall, carrying a stack of magazines.

"I hope those aren't *Playboys*," Joe said.

Owen grinned. "Mechanic magazines."

"Ah, Matt's old stash. So listen. Van says Haley told her you have a grandmother."

"Yeah."

"Do you know where she lives?"

Owen shrugged. "She moved south somewhere."

"South like Cape May or south like Florida?"

"I don't know. Why do you want to know?"

"We thought she might want to know that your mom is in the hospital. She might want to come take care of her."

"No."

"No what?"

"She wouldn't want to come. They had a fight. They were always fighting. Why can't we just stay here?"

"You can." Joe looked at his mother, then at Van. "But don't you want to be home for Santa?"

"Santa, right. That's a joke."

"We should call her—she would want to know," Mom Enthorpe said.

"No, she wouldn't. It sucks where we live. We don't have a tree. Or anything." He turned on Van. "Haley should have kept her big mouth shut. Why did you have to tell on us?"

"I didn't," Van said. "I was trying to help."

"Everything was fine before you came, when Joe was living at the marina. That was the best ever."

"Owen, that's unfair," Mom Enthorpe said. "Joe's job was only temporary and you have to go to school."

"I hate school."

Joe grabbed him by the shoulder. "That's enough. Lashing out isn't helping. Especially lashing out at Van."

Van's stomach lurched. She bit the insides of her cheeks to keep her dinner down. It would be too much for them all to start overreacting right now.

"You don't want us, fine. I'll take the girls home. I can take care of them."

"Young man, show some respect." Granddad Joe came into the room. "Didn't anyone ever tell you not to bite the hand that feeds you?"

"I'll pay you back for the lasagna as soon as I find another job."

Granddad fisted his hands on his hips and laughed. "What? We don't pay you enough?"

"It's not funny."

"The thought of you in a paper hat, asking if I want fries with that just to pay off some lasagna is pretty damn funny. Guess you might as well give all those mechanic magazines back 'cause you aren't gonna have time for studying engines what with your job and taking care of the family."

Owen's face had gradually turned a deep red. From embarrassment, anger or frustration, Van couldn't tell. But she could guess it was a combination of them all. God knows she had been there enough times in her youth to recognize it. Recognize and empathize with everything he said and felt. Even down to blaming her. She'd spent plenty of time blaming others back in the day, she'd spent plenty of time since then blaming herself.

Grandpa frowned, shook his head. "And here I was thinking that once you got out of college or tech school, you'd come to work at the vineyard."

"You did?"

"Weren't we talking about that just the other day?" He looked to his son and grandson.

The other two Joes nodded solemnly.

Van didn't know if they'd really discussed it or they were just giving the kid false hopes. Because she didn't see any way Owen could go to college if something in his family situation didn't change. Kids like Owen were lucky to make it through high school

"Sorry," Owen said. He handed the stack of old magazines back to Granddad.

Granddad shoved his hands in his pants pocket. "I don't want those dirty old things back, but I think you oughta apologize—"

"Girls!" Mom Enthorpe exclaimed, cutting him off. "Here you are—ready for bed already?"

Haley and Kayla stood in the doorway, dressed for bed. Kayla in a faded nightgown that was too small for her. Haley in yoga pants and a stretched-out tank top.

"Teeth brushed?" Mom Enthorpe asked as she crossed the room to where they were standing.

They both shook their heads.

"Well good, because I was thinking some hot chocolate would be just what we needed before bed."

The two girls stepped all the way into the room. Owen shot Haley a dirty look. Haley huffed past him, and he gave her a shove. "Stupid snitch."

She yanked away and lifted her chin but Van could see her lip was trembling.

"Owen!" all three Joes said.

Normally Van would have laughed at the three generations all having the same reaction, but tonight she was suddenly heart sore. Mom Enthorpe did laugh. "Come along, girls," she said and managed to get her arms around Haley and Kayla and Van in one smooth practiced movement.

As Mom trundled the girls toward the kitchen, Van saw Owen break away from Joe and run down the hall. A minute later she heard his door slam.

VAN SNUGGLED AGAINST Joe. As usual when she should be feeling content and happy, she could barely keep her worries at bay. She'd heard Owen and Haley arguing from Haley's room after everyone was in bed.

Van wanted to put her pillow over her head and drown out his words like she had done so many nights of her own childhood. She knew it was just two children, both frightened and hurting. Intellectually she knew she hadn't caused their rift. There was a grandmother who might help the family and from what Joe had learned today when he called the hospital, Kathy Davis would need help once she was released from the hospital. If she was released . . .

"Stop thinking," Joe said against her hair.

"Can't help it."

"I know, but Owen didn't mean what he said to you."

"I wasn't thinking about that, but yes he did."

"Well, maybe at the time but now he's worried that you're mad at him."

"Of course not. I'm an adult."

Joe chuckled and kissed the top of her head.

"Besides . . ."

Joe pulled away to look at her. "Besides what?"

"I know what he's going through."

"You do?"

"Well, not exactly. But about being torn. Wanting your mom, but wanting your mom like it is here, not like it really is. And I'm guessing that having three men in his life who care about him is pretty enticing. Which makes him feel guilty. And . . ."

"You are pretty wise, you know that?"

"Not wise. I just remember wishing the same thing."

Joe pulled her close. "We would have taken you in. We didn't know."

"Water under the bridge. They'll need the extra help when their mother gets out of the hospital. If the grandmother is even willing. Haley said they had a big fight before she left."

"But would Owen really want to stay away from them?" Joe said. "I can't imagine wanting to leave my family. Damn, I'm sorry, Van."

"Stop apologizing."

"Sorry. But I know holidays aren't easy for you. And with all this added hoopla with the kids, I don't want you to hate being here."

"I don't. I'm fine with it all. Why can't you accept that?"

"I can. I will. Let's not fight."

"I'm not fighting. I'm just upset that Owen is taking his hurt out on his sister."

"Oh, that's normal. Siblings say stupid stuff to each other all the time."

"You guys don't."

"That's because we're adults. But you should have heard us back in the day."

"I don't remember you fighting."

"We were always on our best behavior when you came to visit."

Van pushed away so she could look at him. "Why?"

Joe's eyebrows lifted. "Because I threatened them."

"Why?"

"Because I loved you and I didn't want them to frighten you away. And I love you now, Van. And I'm still acting a little clueless, aren't I?"

"A bit."

"Forgive me?"

"Yep." She wrapped her arms around him and held on tight. She loved Joe, she loved his family, she was even beginning to love her father again. Which reminded her she hadn't bought him and his significant other, Ruth, a Christmas present.

She reached for her phone.

"What are you doing?"

"Adding to my Christmas list."

"I want a pony."

"I'll give you something even better than a pony."

She put the phone back on the side table, turned toward him and kissed him. She could have the best of both worlds, the business she'd worked so hard for and the people who loved her and whom she loved.

*Please don't let me screw this up again.*

*Chapter Eight*

---

VAN HEARD THE noise. Just a click. Something outside? She peered out the bedroom window. It was late, quiet and dark.

Again the click. The sound of a door opening and closing? One of the children going to the bathroom. She lay listening. When she didn't hear anything else, she slipped out of bed, went to the door and opened it a crack.

There was a night-light burning in the hallway in case one of the kids woke up. But down the hall, the bathroom door was open and it was dark inside.

Van eased through the door opening and quietly shut it. She wouldn't wake up Joe; she could do this.

She padded down the hall to the bathroom. Looked inside. It was empty. She went back to the girls' room and opened the door enough to peek inside. Kayla was asleep, but Haley's bed was empty. Van looked on the floor, into the corners.

She slipped back into the hallway and thought she saw a movement at the front end of the hall.

It must be Haley, going to the kitchen. Maybe she just needed a glass of water. Van relaxed. She stood for a second, irresolute, then decided this was as good a time as any to have a little talk. But when she opened the kitchen door, the room was dark.

"Haley?"

No answer.

She couldn't be going outside.

Was the girl sleepwalking? Traumatized kids did sometimes. Or had night terrors or other unusual behavior. And what did you do when that happened? Lead them back to bed without waking them up? Wake them up and risk totally freaking them out?

Van didn't have a clue. She should have woken Joe when she first heard something, but it was too late now. She groped her way across the room unwilling to turn on the light and risk startling Haley.

And then she heard the back door open and close. And all thought of going for Joe fled. Van didn't hesitate. Haley was outside alone. There was hardly any moon. She could get hurt or lost. If she was walking in her sleep, her judgment would be nonexistent.

Van considered yelling for help. Dismissed it. She didn't want to alarm anyone. Not yet. She could handle this.

She cautiously followed and realized the girl had taken her coat. Haley wasn't sleep walking. She was running away.

Van's heart stuttered to a stop, freezing her where she stood, as her own dreaded past broke full-blown into the darkness. *No, Haley.* That wasn't the answer.

Van grabbed her own jacket, slipped her feet into Mom Enthorpe's garden clogs and ran after her.

Van could see her now, moving fast, a small shadow sliding and stumbling over the newly fallen snow. And then clouds scudded across the moon, and Van lost sight of her.

She peered down the long drive to the road, but nothing was moving there.

"Haley?" she called, not too loud, she didn't want to frighten her. She knew about being frightened and she knew her first response was *Run* even when she wanted to stay.

Van turned in a full circle. There were a few trees around the house. They created comfortable shade in summer; tonight their branches rose bare in the night, but none of them hid a runaway child.

The outbuildings? She might be hiding in the shadows there.

Had she cut through the woods to the main road or fled over the vineyards where in the dark she would be lost among the rows and rows of vines? Or worse she might get disoriented and wander into the creek where they used to swim.

Van needed help. She turned back toward the house, just as a soft glow appeared in the window of the gift shop. Not the overhead lights, she realized. But the tree lights.

Van let out a breath so full of relief that it nearly knocked her over. She took a couple of calming breaths, surprised at how intense her emotions had been.

Now what? Interfere or watch from the coziness of the kitchen? She only hesitated a second before she strode forward and opened the door.

Haley was sitting on the stone floor, hugging her knees, her face lifted to the lights of the towering tree.

Van gently closed the door. The room was still a little warm from when the crew had been working there earlier. But not warm enough to sit for long.

What was she supposed to do? She didn't know how to make things better for this frightened girl.

Despair and running were things Van knew about and she didn't want to screw this up. One wrong word or reaction could unravel everything. She'd been there herself and even now her instinct was to run, go back to bed, not face whatever demons would come out along with Haley's.

She stopped, surprised at her own thoughts. Run? Maybe. It's what she did. But to bed? That's where she was going to run to? Really?

And in the chasm between wanting to help and wanting to run away, Van had an epiphany and almost laughed out loud. If she was only running as far as back to bed, she'd made some progress in her life.

And if she could make it, surely she could help Haley.

She slipped out of the clogs. No reason to clomp over to your potentially first ever heart-to-heart.

"Mind if I sit down?"

Haley buried her face and shook her head against her knees.

Van started to sit.

"Go away."

*Now what?* Van wondered as she crouched halfway to the floor. "Please?"

Haley sputtered. Her shoulders vibrated beneath her jacket then a ragged sob sprang from her, startling Van into sitting abruptly and putting her arm around the girl.

"Go away, go away, go away," Haley cried between sobs, but since she didn't try to move away or push Van away, Van stayed put.

She didn't have a clue as to what to say. If only someone had followed her out. Like Mom. She'd know exactly what to do to make Haley feel better. Even Granddad would joke her out of it.

But no one came and the two of them sat there.

It was kind of peaceful with the tiny halos of light perching like fireflies among the branches.

Still her rational mind was screaming, *Do something. Say something.* She didn't know where to start. So they sat there side by side, looking up at the tree until Van's neck began to hurt. She shifted on the stone floor. "Isn't your butt getting cold?"

Haley hiccupped. Peeked over at Van with one red-rimmed eye. Nodded.

"You want to go back to the house?"

Haley shook her head and buried her face again.

Van looked around. The boys had really done a good job of clearing the place out. Only the boxes of supplies were left, stacked in the corner. Wine-themed decorations she'd ordered online. Dollars to donuts there would be a Christmas tree skirt in one of the boxes. "Hang on."

She pushed to her feet. Her legs were already stiff from the cold and she hobbled over to the stack of boxes and rummaged through them until she found a bag that said TREE SKRT. She ripped the bag open and detoured to the thermostat to jack up the heat a couple of degrees.

Haley hadn't moved, so Van folded the skirt in half and spread it out on the floor next to her. Haley lifted her butt enough to get onto the skirt.

Van sat down next to her. "This is kind of cozy, huh?"

"You're weird."

"I know. I can't help it."

"Do people like you?"

This was taking a turn she hadn't expected. "I have a few friends."

"I don't."

"I'm sure—" Van clamped down on the reassurance. How lame could she be? "That must suck."

Haley darted her a look. "It does."

"Are you sure you don't have *any*?"

"Just the girls next door and they don't count."

"Why not? Don't you like them?"

"I used to."

"But not now?"

Haley shrugged. "They said we were losers. That we were too poor to get a Christmas tree."

"A lot of people don't have Christmas trees," Van said. "I don't usually get a tree." She was too busy decorating other people's houses to do her own. "Actually last year I did get a bunch of those white branches. They were left over from a client, so I took them home and put them in the umbrella stand by the front door of my apartment. It was sort of like a tree."

"That's pitiful."

"Yeah."

"Did you buy a can of Christmas tree smell to spray around?"

"No. Was that you being sarcastic?"

Haley gave her a look that said it was.

Van breathed in the pungent scent of evergreen. "Can't really duplicate the smell of a real tree, can you?"

Haley shook her head. "You have two trees."

"We do."

"We used to always get a tree. But not this year. Momma said she'd see, but I knew that meant no."

"Well, maybe she really meant that she'd see."

"No she didn't. All she ever does is work and we still don't have any money. We never do anything fun. We don't have nice clothes." Haley hid her face in her hands. "I said I hated her."

"Ah."

"I'm such a bitch."

Van blinked. *How old was this kid?*

"You're not the first kid to say that. I think mothers get that you don't mean it."

"What if I don't get to tell her I didn't mean it? What if she dies? It'll be my fault."

*Holy crap.*

"Did you ever tell your mom you hated her?"

Van thought back. "Probably. I'm pretty sure I did."

"Don't you remember?"

Van shook her head. She remembered telling her dad that she hated him plenty of times when her mom was still alive. After her mom died, she lost her bravura and just tried to stay away from him. Until recently.

"And she still likes you?"

And what to say? *She's dead* might push Haley over the brink. "Look, in the morning we'll ask Mom Enthorpe."

"She knows everything, doesn't she?"

"Seems that way. I think we should go back to the house or we're going to have frostbite on our butts."

Haley got up. Van stuck out her hand for Haley to pull her up, which she did. Van turned down the heat and finally after they both stopped to look once more at the tree lights, she turned them off, too.

The moon had come out and cast the snow into a patchwork of white, grays and blues. The air was so cold that their feet crunched as they walked.

"The air tickles your nose when it's this cold," Haley said.

"It does," said Van. "It really does."

JOE AWOKE WITH a start; Van was gone. The sheet beside him wasn't even warm, which meant she must have been gone for some time. He sat up and peered around the room. No Van. He pushed back the covers and went straight to the window.

Her car was still in the driveway. Thank God.

Then he heard footsteps in the hall. He deliberated about going out to meet her or jumping back in bed and pretending he wasn't being such an idiot.

Then he heard whispers. He cracked the bedroom door open. Van and Haley were standing at the doorway of the girls' room. Haley went inside and Van followed her.

Joe padded barefoot down the hall.

"You don't have to be afraid, Haley."

"I'm not."

"I know. Just, sometimes when *I'm* afraid, I know I'm safe here. Good-night."

"Night."

Joe meant to creep away but he wasn't fast enough.

Van's words had sucker punched him. He didn't want her to ever be afraid again.

Van backed out of the room, shut the door and turned right into him.

"What—?"

Van put her fingers to her lips and brushed past him. He followed her to their bedroom and shut the door. "What was that all about?"

Van shivered uncontrollably, jumped into bed and pulled the covers up to her chin. "I heard her get out of bed. I thought she was getting water so I went to help. But she didn't stop at the kitchen. I followed her out to the gift shop."

Joe pushed the pillows against the headboard and climbed in beside her. "Why?"

"Why did I follow her?"

"Why did she go there?"

"To look at the tree, I think. She had a fight with her mom about a Christmas tree, and she told her mom she hated her. Owen is giving her a hard time. She's afraid her mom is going to die. She isn't, is she?"

"No, at least I don't think so. Dad is trying to find the grandmother since we don't get a lot of information about Kathy's condition from the hospital. What did you tell her?"

"Not much. I said that all kids told their mothers that and it doesn't mean anything. And that your mom would explain everything in the morning."

Joe laughed in spite of the gravity of the situation.

"Well I wasn't going to say, 'Everything will be all right,' because it might not be. Then she'd never trust anyone again."

Joe pulled her close and she leaned her head on his shoulder.

"There wasn't much I could say. I didn't want to tell her that my mom was dead. It might make her feel worse. And remembering how I felt about my dad just made me feel worse, so I didn't say anything."

"Did you mean it about her not having to be afraid here?"

"Of course. Would your family turn them away?"

He shook his head. "What about you?"

"Would I turn them away? It isn't my house."

"We'll debate that later. But would you, if it was?"

She shook her head. "How could I? You didn't turn me away."

And he never would. No matter how infuriatingly skittish she was. But the question was, could he keep her?

## *Chapter Nine*

WHEN VAN CAME into the kitchen the next morning, Mom and Kayla were the only ones there.

"I guess I overslept," Van said.

"You sleep as long as you need," Mom said, putting a mug of coffee at her place. Van sat down. She already had her own place at the table, she realized. She'd sat in the same place fifteen years ago.

It was tempting to believe everything would work out fine. Across from her Kayla was eating a bowl of cereal. With each bite a little milk dribbled down the front of her sweatshirt.

Van resisted the urge to walk around and stick a napkin under her chin. Children were messy. She'd have to get used to it if she and Joe were going to adopt.

She stopped, coffee mug halfway to her lips. Slowly she put the mug down.

"Are you all right, Van? You suddenly look very pale." Mom put her palm against Van's forehead. "No temp."

"Just tired," Van managed. Had she actually just thought about adoption? On her own? Thinking about the future with Joe without fighting it? Even if they did get married, they couldn't live with Mom and Joe Jr. and Granddad forever. And how on earth would Van figure out how to take care of children on her own? Especially with her business and the winery to run?

*Stop fighting it.*

*Leave me alone.*

She wanted things to take their course, sort of. Since she'd left home all those years before, she'd made sure she was in control of her life. Managed every detail while still being able to see the whole picture.

Now all that was going out the window. But could she make that final no-going-back step?

Mom poured herself more coffee and on her way to her place at the table, she managed to pick up a napkin, wipe it across Kayla's face and stick it under her chin without slowing down—or so it seemed to Van.

*While you were sitting here thinking about doing it.* How could she ever be a wife and mother—adoptive mother?

The kitchen door opened.

"Well, look who's awake," Mom said.

Haley stood in the doorway, hair straggly, face puffy, eyes focused on the floor.

"Come sit down, honey. Do you want cereal? Or would you rather have some eggs or oatmeal?"

Haley shrugged.

Mom reached over and pulled out the chair next to Kayla's.

Haley glanced at it, hesitated a little longer. "Cereal, please." And she walked to the opposite side of the table and sat down next to Van.

Mom started to get up.

"I'll get it," Van said and jumped up. She got a bowl down from the cabinet and placed it in front of Haley. Pulled the milk carton closer to her.

Van sat down again.

Haley poured cereal, then milk, her eyes never wavering from the bowl.

Van glanced at Mom Enthorpe, who quirked one side of her mouth.

Van had to admit she was a little relieved. After last night she wasn't sure whether Haley would reject her for letting her see too much of her vulnerability. Next day remorse. Boy, could Van relate.

"Where are the guys?" Van asked.

"They went out with the snowplow earlier then called to say they had a few errands to do. I've given up on haircuts, so who knows?"

"Actually, I thought if you don't need me, I might do a little last-minute shopping."

"Sure. You go have a good time."

Van glanced over at Haley who was concentrating on her cereal.

"You feel like a little light shopping?" Van asked.

At first Haley didn't move, then slowly she turned her head to look at Van. "Me?"

"Yeah, you."

"I don't have any money."

"Doesn't matter. I've got plastic."

IT WAS COLDER than all get out, Joe thought as he and the other two Joes followed Owen in and out of the stand of evergreens. Every time Owen paused, they paused, every time he struck off again they followed.

They were taking a tree to the Davis house to surprise their mother when she returned home. The hospital had located their grandmother, Charlise. Joe hadn't mentioned that to Owen or the girls. No one was sure if she would actually show up to take the kids home. Or take care of their mother during her recuperation. They'd all have to wait and see.

Joe started thinking about a hot cup of coffee. His father mumbled something about Florida and the newspaper.

Granddad just chuckled. "Come on, ya wusses."

Several trees later, Owen stopped. "This one."

"Great," Joe said.

"Nah, that's lame," said Granddad. "This one is better."

"That one's too big," Owen said. "It won't fit in our living room."

"How about this one?" Joe said. "It's tall but skinny."

The four guys consulted. Agreed. Joe handed Owen

the axe, positioned his hands on the handle. "Now re-member what I told you."

Owen nodded. Planted his feet on either side of the tree trunk.

"Don't cut off any toes," Granddad said and stepped out of range.

Joe gave him a look.

While Owen chopped, Granddad kibitzed and gave advice while Joe and his dad watched from the sidelines.

"You're going to miss him when he goes back home," his father said.

"Yes," Joe agreed. He was sort of surprised at how much.

"And if his mother isn't in a condition to take care of him or the girls? Or worse?"

"I don't know. Owen would want to stay with us. I don't know about the girls, but . . ." Joe shrugged.

"Is that what you want?"

"I don't know. It would be a big step."

"What does Van say about it?"

"We haven't really discussed it."

"Well, that's something the two of you need to re-solve before you go much further."

"I know, I'm just so afraid of hurting her feelings or driving her away."

His father slapped him on the back. "Better to find out now than later. But let me give you a little advice. I think you and Van would make a good life together. But don't force things."

"You mean wait?"

"I mean don't spring everything you want on her all at once. Life together is a compromise, always." His father grinned. "With you doing most of the compromising."

"Timber!" Granddad yelled as the tree cracked, and fell softly onto the snow.

"Good job." Joe took the axe from Owen and handed it to his granddad.

Granddad chuckled, obviously having a great time. He swung the axe over his shoulder.

Joe Jr. flinched and took it from him. "Come on you two, let's get that tree on the truck before it starts dropping needles and my behind freezes off. We'll stop by the hardware store and pick up some lights and things on the way to Owen's house. You remembered to bring the key?"

"Yes, sir." Owen patted his pocket.

"And after that, haircuts."

The other two Joes and Owen groaned.

"Like I said, son, compromise."

Joe laughed. He knew his dad was right. There were no guarantees in life.

"I ACTUALLY KIND of hate shopping," Van confessed as she waited for a parking space in downtown Whisper Beach. She'd nixed the mall after two traffic lights of gridlock.

"I wouldn't," Haley said. "Besides, you have all these neat clothes and everything."

"Well, thanks." Van was wearing designer jeans, a black cashmere sweater and a ballerina-pink down jacket she'd bought at the end of last season at Blooming-dale's. She'd "dressed up" mainly because she'd been wearing sweats or Levi's for the past few weeks as she set up shop at Elite Lifestyle Managers and the winery. And because it felt festive. Sort of. She realized her idea of festive wasn't up to snuff. And she planned to remedy that today.

They got out of the car, paid the meter and stepped over the snow that had collected at the curb. Then they stood on the sidewalk looking up and down the street.

Whisper Beach was a beach town, where trendy boutiques rubbed addresses with souvenir and beach stores. In winter, they leaned toward gifts for the holidays and to Van's mind, stuff that people didn't really need.

The nearest shop was one of those. Its window was crammed with seasonal gifts; just looking at it made Van's fingers itch to minimalize and rearrange it. It would be much more effective if they'd just—

"Are we going in?"

"Sorry. What do you think about Santa ties for the guys?"

Haley rolled her eyes and opened the door. They squeezed in at the same time, upending a laugh from Haley. Van grabbed a basket and they went immediately to the tie display that was arranged on a round table in the middle of an alcove of everything imaginable.

"Let's see . . ." Van began. "Elves for . . ."

"Granddad Enthorpe."

"Right." Van dropped the tie into the basket.

"How about this?"

"A reindeer head sticking out of a chimney."

"Owen," they both agreed.

"And here's one of Santa kissing Mrs. Claus," Van said. "That's perfect for Joe Jr."

"What about Joe?"

Van grinned. "Look at this." She held up a bright blue tie with a decorated tree topped by a big star.

"He did cut down the trees," Haley said dubiously.

"But wait," Van said. She fiddled with the back of the tie. The star lit up and began to blink.

"Cool."

The tie went into the basket with the others.

"Do you think there's something for Mom . . . Enthorpe here?" Haley asked.

Van nodded. "Something for Mom Enthorpe and something for your Mom."

Haley cast a quick look at Van, and that quick look said it all. Van swallowed an unwelcome lump in her throat.

"Actually why don't we go someplace a little nicer? Maybe a scarf or jewelry or something."

They spent a few more minutes just looking at all the merchandise. Plastic snow globes with little churches in them, cellophane packages of mistletoe, cocktail napkins with disparaging quotes about Rudolph's red nose.

Haley seemed enthralled with everything and Van realized that the three Davis kids might be spending Christmas at the Enthorpes. Had anyone thought about presents for them? Santa? It looked like she'd have to make another clandestine trip to the store before Christmas.

Van paid for the ties and they moved on to the next store.

"I need to get something to wear that's . . . you know, more Christmassy," Van said. "How about you?"

Haley shrugged. Van knew she was about to step into uncharted territory here. She'd love to buy the girls Christmas dresses, but maybe they had them at home already.

Well, they could always use them for something else.

"I know a store down the street where they have pretty decent clothes." And a children's department, though she wasn't sure what size Haley might be. She was small but not exactly little-kid-sized. If she'd been smart she would have asked Mom Enthorpe all these questions before they'd left. She made a mental note to do so in the future. If there was a future with Haley. She and Owen and Kayla might drift out of their lives as quickly as they'd come. The thought left her oddly deflated.

They passed several stores, with Haley slowing down to look into the decorated windows. Van slowed down to look, too. They didn't have to hurry. Mom Enthorpe had the party preparations under control and everyone was bringing dishes. It would be a feast.

They stopped at the women's clothing store window. On one side of the door the window was filled with cocktail dresses and party clothes; the other side with girls' and children's wear. Van cast a quick eye over the adult side. Really? Black was the main choice for a Christmas party?

Van had plenty of black. It was all she usually wore. Since returning to Whisper Beach she'd tried to color up her wardrobe. No way was she regressing to black for the holidays.

She crossed over to where Haley was checking out a red, black and white yoga pants and tunic ensemble. A nice compromise. "That's pretty cool," Van said tentatively. Since the Davis kids had been staying with them, Van hadn't noticed any discernable style choices. Maybe Joe had packed their clothes and just hadn't chosen well.

Maybe she should call him and find out.

*Or maybe you should just figure this out on your own.*

They went inside. Haley led the way and Van expected her to go right to the kids' department, but she didn't. Several feet in, she stopped, turned to Van.

"What?" Van asked.

"Nothing."

*Okay.* "Why don't we pick out a bunch of stuff then go try them on together?"

Haley frowned. "Me?"

"Yes, you."

"I can get something?"

"Yes. Are we shopping til we're dropping? Or not?"

Haley made a face. "You're weird."

"One of my best qualities. So . . . do you know what size you wear?"

"Small."

Van lowered her chin and raised her eyebrows. "As in not medium or large?"

Haley made a half shrug.

"I think we need a salesperson." Van looked around, there were several. A middle-aged woman, ringing up a purchaser, a young woman refolding tee-shirts and looking bored and another younger woman, who looked slightly hipper than the other two. Van caught her eye and she came over.

"May I help you?"

"We're looking for her size, but we don't know it."

"Ah, let's see." She looked at Haley then riffled through the rack of dresses. She held one up to Haley. "I'd say size eight. Depends on the designer. Some run small, some run true to size."

Van nodded, smiled, thought, *TMI*. She took the dress.

"Now if you're interested in leggings, we have some really cute ones over here." Van and Haley followed her toward another rack of clothes. The saleslady went through the same holding-up process. Chose the size.

"Thanks. That's a great help. I think we can take it from here."

The saleslady smiled. "Just let me know if you have any more questions."

Van smiled. Turned to Haley. "See anything you like?

And don't shrug. Just yes or no. I'm not good at subtlety, especially when it comes to shopping."

Haley screwed up her mouth, looked around. "That." She pointed to the outfit they'd seen displayed in the window.

"What about a dress for the Christmas party and another for Christmas morning?" Van knew immediately from Haley's expression she'd said the wrong thing and hurried on. "Or for some other time. Why don't you pick out a few things and we'll see what you like best?"

The cloud passed and soon Haley was picking out different clothes and Van breathed a sigh of relief.

The saleslady came back and took the clothes to put in a dressing room and Van and Haley moved on to the women's department. Van picked out several dresses for the party and a couple of sweaters that were festive without being gaudy. Really, she had to draw the line somewhere.

"Okay, man your dressing rooms," Van said.

Haley gave her a look before disappearing into the dressing room next to Van's.

"Yell, if you need help,' Van called as an afterthought.

"I'm okay."

*Good*, thought Van. She was already exhausted.

They came out simultaneously. Looked at each other, shook their heads and went back inside. Repeated this so many times that Van was beginning to despair, but at the end of half an hour, they both had chosen two outfits and headed for the cashier.

"What about Kayla?" Haley asked.

"Right. What do you think she would like?"

"That one." Haley pointed to a red empire-waist velvet dress with gold smocking embellished with little pearls across the top.

Van went over to the rack. Pulled one off the bar. "Does this look like the right size?"

Haley frowned and Van was about to put the dress back when she said, "Yes. You're getting better at this."

"Thanks." Van added the dress to the others and dropped them on the counter.

They carried their packages outside. "I'm glad you came with me," Van said. "How about lunch?"

They ate in the local luncheonette, dropped by Untermeyer's Five-and-Dime, which had managed to survive all the gentrification of the downtown area, bought some goofy gifts and four reindeer antler headbands "for the girls" that Haley and Van wore out of the store.

They got back in the car and Van turned on the radio, fiddling with the tuner until she found a Christmas station, and they headed for home.

By the time they pulled into the driveway they were on ten lords-a-leaping of the "Twelve Days of Christmas" and the first snowflakes began to fall.

"We should have bought you a warmer coat. Kayla, too. I'm—"

"No." Haley yanked the reindeer antlers from her head. "I don't want this, none of it. You're not my mom."

"What? Where did that come from?"

But Haley had pushed open the door and was getting out.

Oh man, how had she not noticed what had been happening? She was trying to give Haley a fun day, not supplant her mom. She saw it clear as day now.

Van got out of the car.

Haley was running toward the house.

"Haley, wait. I don't want to be your mother!"

The front door opened and Haley slipped inside.

Haley was gone, but Joe stood in the doorway, staring back at Van, and blocking her way back in.

## Chapter Ten

For an eternity Van and Joe stood looking at each other. She knew what he must be thinking, but how could she explain that she'd only meant that she wasn't trying to take Kathy Davis's place. That she understood that no matter how weird your life got, your mom would always be your mom, even if you couldn't be with her, even after she was dead and you found out she wasn't the perfect person you thought she was.

She just wanted to be a friend, make the journey a little easier, let Haley know that she wasn't alone. That you had to be tough but you could also accept help and love. All the things she was just learning in these last few months. And she'd botched it.

But the look on Joe's face . . . She'd never be able to explain this to him.

He started to move toward her and she panicked.

She jumped back in the car and began to back away. But it was too late; he'd already reached the car.

*Don't lose it. Don't make a scene*, she told herself. *Don't make everyone else unhappy.*

He knocked on the passenger window.

*Don't make a scene.* She let the window down.

"What happened?"

She smiled ruefully. "Too much chocolate and candy canes?"

He frowned at her. And she wanted to kiss it away. She knew that expression like it was her own, the confusion, the worry. She didn't think she could last much longer without having a meltdown just like Haley.

"Then come inside."

He started to open the door.

She slammed on the locks. "I have more errands."

"But it's getting dark and it's starting to snow again."

"Then you better let me go, because I still have things I have to do."

"Do them tomorrow."

"Tomorrow will be all-day party prep and I need to do them today."

"I'll come with you."

"No, it's Christmas."

Finally his expression lightened. "Is this Santa related? Because Dad and I went today just in case the kids' mom doesn't get home for Christmas." He winced. "Sorry."

"Stop it, Joe, just stop it." She stopped herself, took

a breath. "If you want anything under the tree, you'd better let me get to the store before it closes. Scoot."

He let go of the car and she backed away before he could change his mind.

When she reached the end of the drive he was still watching her. He waved as she pulled onto the road; she honked as she drove away, just like any normal day. It didn't feel normal.

She slowed down at the curve in the road and looked back through the trees to where the lights on the Christmas boughs festooned across the eaves of the farmhouse looked like a Christmas card. *The symbol of idyllic happiness.*

No. Not idyllic, but a place for affection and squabbles, hard times and happy times. Early mornings, backbreaking work, hearty meals prepared in love. And so much more. There was a place for her here, if only she was sure they wouldn't grow to regret welcoming her to the family.

She drove on. She meant to stop at Dorie's, get some kick-in-the-butt advice from the woman who had never failed her and whom Van hoped she'd at least begun to repay.

But there were no cars in the driveway. Of course. It was the dinner rush and Dorie and Dana would be at the Blue Crab. Suze's car was gone, too. Probably out doing last-minute shopping. That would be so much like Suze, to put off everything until Chaucer let go of her and she remembered there were only two more days before Christmas.

She drove to where the next block ended at the boardwalk. A half block north the Blue Crab's new sign shone through the increasing snowfall. There were cars already parked along the boardwalk. Excellent. Van had known business would boom if Dorie would only spruce up the restaurant and open during the off season. It had been hard, but once Dorie was convinced, she'd thrown herself full force into the renovation.

Van turned toward the restaurant but didn't stop until several parking spaces beyond it. She cut the engine and just sat in the quiet, looking out at the sea while darkness fell and she could no longer tell the sand from the snow.

Then she got out of the car, zipped up her jacket and walked down the wooden steps to the beach.

JOE STOOD WATCHING as Van drove away. He knew in his gut that she wasn't going shopping. It was just an excuse to get away from him. Them.

He went back in the house, feeling sick and knowing he was missing something essential. Something of life-changing importance, and he worried that his chance of figuring it out had just driven away.

His mother was down the hall with Haley, so he sat down with his father and granddad and waited. None of them spoke when she finally came back to the living room alone. She didn't sit down but stood facing them.

They all sat a little straighter.

Joe opened his mouth to ask what happened, but a look from his mother stopped him.

"Now we're going to have a little talk, but I'm going to do the talking for a change."

They waited.

"The holidays can be a stressful time for everyone. But especially if your mother is in the hospital and you're staying with strangers. No, Joe, don't interrupt me."

Joe didn't know which Joe she was talking to, so he kept his mouth shut.

"And especially if you're not used to celebrating the season. There's not much we can do for those children except make them feel welcome. But we can give Van a place to enjoy the holidays. Think about it. She's been working nonstop since she came back. Setting up the vineyard financials, getting the gift shop ready for the party, starting her own business. Participating in the family, buying presents, making cookies, dealing with three children we didn't expect."

"I shouldn't have brought them," Joe said. "I didn't know she would freak."

"As for freaking out, I don't think Van has ever freaked out in her life." His mother huffed out an exasperated sigh. "Joe—and Joe and Joe—I love you all dearly and I know you all want what's best, but you can't push people into being what you want when you want it."

"What did we do?" Granddad asked.

"You, for one, keep dropping wedding hints every chance you get."

"And why not? When you get a good one, you don't want to let them get away, right, son?"

Both Joe and his dad nodded.

Mom laughed, but he knew she wasn't finished. "Joe and Van have issues they need to resolve before they go any further."

Joe looked down. He loved his family but he didn't really want to listen to his personal life laid bare.

"Hell, if you're talking about kids," Granddad continued, "we got plenty already. And we'll be good with whatever you decide. Just look how those three have taken to her."

"But Haley came home crying," Joe said. "And Van yelled at her."

His mother threw her head back, not a gesture they saw often, it was about as outwardly upset she ever got.

They braced themselves.

"Your granddad is right at least about the last part. Owen totally gets her."

Joe nodded. He did and Van got him.

"And Haley is in there crying her eyes out because she was having such a good time with Van that she forgot about her mother being sick and in the hospital. Van was trying to reassure her, not push her away."

"Damn," said Joe.

"That's not language for the holiday."

"Sorry. I didn't understand what was happening."

"You didn't take the time to understand."

"She drove away before I could."

"Maybe she needed a moment to regroup. But there you were, asking her what was wrong or trying to make her feel better. Sometimes a woman doesn't need a man."

His father gasped.

"You're not being funny, Joseph."

"You're in trouble now," his granddad said under his breath.

"And so are you." Mom turned to Joe. "You're so worried that things aren't going to work out that if you're not careful, you're going to drive her away for good."

Joe knew she was right. He ran his fingers through his hair.

"Don't be so hard on the boy," his dad said. "We were all guilty of it. But da—arn, she's one of the family already."

"To us," his mother said in a much quieter voice. "The Enthorpes are wonderful but sometimes a daunting force of nature. It's hard when you're the new girl in the family. I remember and I didn't even have Van's issues."

"I'm such an idiot," Joe said.

"But you're a lovable idiot. And she loves you."

"I'm going after her."

"Joe."

"No, Mom, I waited the last time and I didn't see her for twelve years. I'm not taking that chance again."

She nodded and handed him his jacket. "Don't try too hard."

He nodded. She turned him around and buttoned

his jacket like he was about Owen's age. "You'd better have the best Christmas present in the world."

"I do. I hope." He kissed her and left.

His mother was probably right. Van might need a little space, but Joe wasn't taking any chances this time. Twelve years ago he'd sulked, intending to forgive her for doubting him once he'd gotten over being mad at her.

He'd never gotten the chance; by the time he tried to apologize she had left Whisper Beach and him for good. He hadn't known until last summer what had really driven her away. He'd be damned if he'd lose her again.

He drove straight to Van's old house, the new office of Elite Lifestyle Managers. Even in the dark, the house looked like a different place. Not a place filled with dark memories and unhappiness, but a place with a future as only Van Moran could make it.

It was also clear that she wasn't there.

He drove through downtown, wipers brushing the snowflakes from the windshield. The sidewalks were busy and there was hardly a parking place to be had, but he didn't see her car.

Now what? He doubted very seriously that Van would take on the mall tonight. And if she was driving back to Manhattan in this weather, he'd call Jerry Corso to get the police after her.

He drove toward the beach. If she was hanging out anywhere it would be at Dorie's. But when he arrived, Dorie's was dark except for the porch light and there were no cars out front.

The last time he'd done this, he'd parked across the street and waited for he didn't know what. But that night there had been cars and lights and just as he was about to give up and leave, the door opened, Van stepped onto the porch and came down the steps.

He'd followed her to the beach, staying behind so she wouldn't know he was there.

*The beach*. Of course. He drove on, turned left at the boardwalk and drove past the Blue Crab. There was her car parked at Whisper Beach.

It's where they'd spent their early years; the little delta of beach between the pier and the river that tourists ignored in favor of the wide white beaches south of the pier. The locals' beach, where once a pirate's mistress had come to watch for his return while she hushed her baby to the sounds of the waves.

Joe laughed; he'd forgotten all about that stupid legend. The dude had never come back. No one knew what happened to the mistress and her baby—if they even existed. Probably none of it was true.

He parked next to Van's car and got out. Walked across the boardwalk and leaned on the rail, the full déjà vu of last summer seeping over him. Only then it wasn't snowing, the moon had been out and he could see her silhouette as she walked by the tide.

Still, he saw her. Even through the snowfall, even though she was partially hidden by the pier, he knew it was Van.

That night, he'd crept away, embarrassed and feeling

like a voyeur. Tonight he climbed down the steps to the sand.

He wasn't sure what he was going to say. He just walked across the beach, his mind blank. The whole drive he'd thought about what he would say. And he hadn't even managed to come up with an opening line.

She didn't hear him as he approached. Or maybe she did, because she didn't seem at all surprised when he stepped up beside her.

He said the first thing that came to his mind. "I'm sorry."

She turned her head to give him a signature Van look, a mix of strength, pain, humor, exasperation and irony that only she could pull off. "Is Haley better?"

"Yeah. Mom said she was feeling guilty for having such a good time."

Van nodded.

"You knew what she was feeling, didn't you?"

She shrugged, or maybe it was a sigh, because her pink puffy jacket just rose and fell.

"Yeah, it took me a second but then I remembered. It's so unfair to dangle the carrot of your family to them. The cookies, the presents, the shopping trip."

"What are you talking about?"

"She has a home, a family, and it may be tough and not as comfortable and easy as ours, but it's her family. And Owen's and Kayla's. I know you can't understand that."

He moved closer.

"When I was younger, it was great being at the farm with all of you. But it made going home all that much harder, so hard that sometimes I tried to make myself not come, but I couldn't stay away. I just kept coming back."

"You could have stayed."

"No, I couldn't. I had a family, as unloving as it was between my mother and father. And after she died, who would take care of my father if I didn't?"

"But you did run away."

"He kicked me out and then it was too late to come to you."

He slipped his arm around her.

"Those children have a mother who loves them. So I'm not being mean to Haley when I tell her I don't want to take her mother's place. Or if I'm hard on Owen. I want them to survive and to think they have a chance, but not by giving them false hopes or taking them away from their mother."

"I didn't think that. I was just worried that if she died . . ."

"That would be a different situation, but she isn't going to die."

He put both arms around her and she slipped easily in front of him. They stared out at the water, silent.

"You know I followed you down here when you first got back last summer?"

She twisted to look up at him.

"You did?"

"I was sitting in my truck outside Dorie's trying to

get the nerve to knock on the door, when you came out. I watched you go down the sidewalk and I followed you."

"I knew someone was there! Jeez, I thought you might be a psychopath or something."

"I know—that's why I skulked away. Plus I was afraid I might get arrested. What were you doing down here?"

"Remembering."

"What?"

"The story about the pirate's mistress."

He'd just been thinking of it himself. "What made you think about that?"

"Well, the girls used to come down beneath the pier and whisper to the surf the name of the boy they wanted to marry."

"I hope you said, 'Joe.'"

"Hmm, I'm trying to remember."

Joe let go of her long enough to cup his hands over his mouth. "She said, 'Joe!'" he yelled above the waves. "'Joe!' She said 'Joe!'"

Van laughed. "You crazy person."

"Crazy about you. Even though your hair is covered in snow."

"So is yours."

He shook his head, dislodging the flakes. "Will you come home now?"

"I still have errands."

"You can do them tomorrow. I've got hot chocolate," he tempted.

He followed her home. The house was quiet and they had their hot chocolate and some broken cookies in the kitchen alone.

Joe was pretty sure they had just reached some understanding, he wasn't sure what, but he wasn't going to push it. Tomorrow was Christmas Eve. They were together and that was enough for him.

## *Chapter Eleven*

EVERYONE WAS UP early the next morning, plowing the walk and drive and plying it with deicer; setting up buffet tables in the winery and festooning the doorways with pine and holly and lights. Even Owen, Haley and Kayla helped.

Haley hadn't spoken to Van that morning. A couple of times their eyes had caught and Haley gave her a half smile.

Van got it and it was all the acknowledgment she needed.

It was Owen who actually came up to her, looking downcast and embarrassed.

Was Joe making him apologize? She didn't want that.

"Hey, dude, dope party?"

He looked up and grinned. "Dope."

"So can you give me a hand with this box? I think it needs four hands."

"Sure." They carried a box of rented champagne flutes over to the drinks table. Even though it was a largely symbolic, a one-glass toast to the holidays, it was an Enthorpe tradition since they didn't party on New Year's Eve, but stayed at home to start their next year among family.

By two o'clock the chafing dishes were lined up along the tables awaiting the myriad of dishes being kept warm or cold in the kitchen. The newly installed "facilities" were polished to a shine, the cloak room was stocked with matching heavy duty hangers and boot racks.

"A real transformation," Joe Jr. said. "And in such a short time."

Van nodded. Thanks to the Enthorpe men and the off-season workers who lived in the farm-hand bunks across the road. It had cost a bit more than they'd wanted to spend, but she also knew that quality won out and she was pleased with the results.

"All right, everyone," Mom called out. "Great job, see you back here for the party. Girls—and boys—let's go get dressed."

They were met by the sound of several cars coming to a stop outside.

"She does that every year," Joe Jr. said. "I swear they must call ahead and tell her they're coming."

"Just good planning," Mom said, and took his arm as they went outside to meet the rest of the family. Even Duffy, who had found a cozy sleeping corner, pushed to his stiff old legs and padded across the floor, tail wagging lazily behind him.

The rest of the Enthorpes were piling out of cars and trucks.

"Told you we'd be back in plenty of time for the party," Dave said, giving his mother a hug. Matt, Dave and Elizabeth had taken what they called their combination graduation, end of exams and bring-along-little-brother ski trip. They were tanned and colorful in their skiwear and full of energy.

They were followed by Brett and his wife, Wendy, and their kids. The only ones missing were Drew, stationed in the air force in Berlin, and Maddy whose family was spending Christmas with her in-laws in Ohio.

Later in the afternoon, the other guests would arrive, along with the more distant Enthorpe relations, who would appear like a small nation to celebrate, then disappear again until the next family function.

Everyone bustled into the house where an urn of coffee was warming.

"Good to have the family, well most of 'em anyway, home again," Granddad said. "That includes you, Van. In case you're wondering."

"Thanks." Van stood on tiptoe and kissed his cheek.

"Hey, hey," he laughed. "That's my girl."

Van waited for the usual quip about marrying Joe

but it didn't follow. He took her arm and they joined the others going into the house.

Coffee was served and hors d'oeuvres were passed while Mom admonished them not to eat all the party food, which was ridiculous. There was enough food to feed an army or two and Van knew Dorie would be bringing even more from the restaurant.

Van started to leave to change into her new Christmas dress; she looked around for Joe and found him looking out the front window, not for the first time that day.

"Expecting someone special?"

"I don't know."

"Anyone I know? Is Santa making an appearance by any chance?"

"He always does." He turned and smiled at her. "But he usually flies."

"Ah, got it," Van said, glancing at Brett and Wendy's kids inspecting packages beneath the tree. She wondered if Haley still believed in Santa. She doubted if Owen did, which was a real shame.

She went down the hall, heard the girls in their room. She would have liked to poke her head in to see if they needed help, but she didn't dare. She'd sensed a tenuous peace between her and Haley and she didn't want to risk upsetting her again.

So she went to her own room and took a long look at her new dress.

It was so not her. She took her standby black out of

the closet and hung it next to the new dress. It was what she knew, comfortable but elegant. She knew who she was in that black dress.

It took some doing but finally she put on the new dress. Changed her earrings. Slipped her feet into heels and was just leaving her room when Joe came in to change. He stopped in the doorway and stared.

"What?"

"You look . . ."

"Like a Christmas tree?"

"Like an emerald," he said. "Unless you were going for the tree look."

She laughed. "Emerald will do."

"Wanna stay here and skip the party?"

She pushed him away. "Get dressed. I'll wait for you in the living room. And I suggest you wash your face, you have tomato sauce on your cheek."

He laughed. "That's not sauce, it's Aunt Harriett's lipstick, but advice taken."

She kissed his other cheek and left him to it.

BY THE TIME Joe and Van stepped out of the house to walk across the drive to the party, the parking area and both sides of the drive were packed with cars, and the soon-to-be gift shop was abuzz with revelers.

"We may have to expand before we even open," Joe said to her.

Van crossed her eyes at him. "At least wait til spring."

"Beep, beep, wide load coming through."

Van knew that voice; she turned around. "Dorie!"

Dorie Lister, wearing her "Sunday" pearls over a red Santa sweater, was coming up the drive holding a huge chafing dish of her famous Blue Crab specialty. It seemed to Van that Dorie never got older, just more Dorie. Skinny "as a ladder" and "twice as creaky," according to her.

"No time for hugs and kisses til later, I gotta get these crab balls to a hot plate."

"Here, let me take those for you," Joe said.

"Har. Think I was born yesterday? You'd have half of them eaten before they got to the buffet table."

Dorie wriggled her way past them while Dana Mulvanney, the transformed bad girl of Whisper Beach High, holding another tray just as large, followed in her wake.

"Would you get a load of Dana?" Joe said.

"I know," Van said. "I hardly recognized her without the spiked hair. But curls?"

"It looks kind of funny," Joe said as they went inside.

"Don't you dare laugh at her."

"I wouldn't think of it," he said, and promptly burst into laughter.

"I'm pretending I don't know you," Van said and walked away to greet some newcomers.

Across the room she saw Mom Enthorpe and Joe Jr. talking with friends. Haley and Kayla stood next to them dressed in their new dresses. They were so cute

Van wanted to hug both of them. She didn't but she did wander nonchalantly their way. "You girls look great!" she said, probably with way too much enthusiasm. But so what? It was Christmas and they did look great.

"Thank you, thank you for my dress," Kayla said.

"Thanks," Haley said with way less enthusiasm, but she couldn't keep from breaking into a smile, which she quickly extinguished.

It was enough. "Well, enjoy. I'm going to go get a glass of something I can have since I don't have to drive."

She left them and made the rounds, even stopping to talk to Dana.

"I like the new do," she said.

Dana shrugged. "Wanted to try something different. You know, stop scaring the customers with the Goth look."

"Good thinking, I like it."

"Thanks. Holy crap. Look who just came in, and she has a date that isn't Jerry."

Van looked up to see Suze shrugging out of something that looked like a medieval monk's cape to reveal a long-sleeve white-and-gold midi dress.

"She's wearing heels," Van said.

"Forget the heels, that dress is going to look like carnage in a snowfield before the party is over."

"Who is the guy she's with?"

"Beats me," said Dana. "Maybe they met in the parking lot."

Or maybe Suze had finally given in to her mother's

choice of suitable men. Suze saw them and steered her companion through the crowd toward them. They did hugs and air kisses and Suze introduce her friend.

"This is Xavier Sendoa."

"Yikes," Dana said under her breath. "Double yikes."

"He's a fellow of physics at Princeton."

Xavier nodded solemnly. "Which is a position conducive to fascinating party conversation and alliteration."

*He's perfect*, Van thought. "A colleague," she said, as they shook hands.

"Yes. Though we never met until my parents insisted I accompany them to the Turner's holiday party."

Suze grinned at Van and reached across her for a ham-wrapped asparagus.

"He also writes poetry." Suze took a bite and Van just managed to catch the dollop of remoulade before it christened Suze's new dress.

She handed Suze a napkin, licked excess remoulade off her finger and turned her attention back to Xavier. He was tall, taller than Suze, whippet thin with a sonorous voice and dressed in an expensive but ill-fitting suit. There was a mustard stain on the *lapel*.

*A match made in heaven.* "I'm so happy to meet you," Van said.

"Likewise. I've heard so much about you all."

Jerry Corso stepped up to the group. "Yo, girls. How's it going?" He glanced quickly at Dana and away.

"Nice to meet you, Xavier," Dana said. "See ya around, Jerry." She walked away.

Jerry sighed.

Suze rolled her eyes. "'Yo'? That's the best you could do? 'Yo'?"

"You said to be cool."

"I said suave."

"Same thing."

"No it isn't," Van, Suze and Xavier said simultaneously.

"Okay, suave. Yeah, like suave. I got it. Suave." Jerry wandered away in Dana's direction.

"Good luck with that one," Van said.

Joe joined them and introductions were made again. More people arrived, and each time the door opened, Joe looked toward it.

It was getting late when two women Van didn't recognize walked in and stood just inside the doorway.

"At last," Joe said and hurried to meet them.

Van automatically followed him. She met Mom and Joe Jr. and Granddad headed in the same direction and heard the first shrill cry.

"Momma!" Kayla appeared out of the crowd and rushed toward the woman who Van realized was being supported by her companion. Then Owen and Haley were running, too.

Kathy Davis, dwarfed by a down jacket, opened her arms and Van thought, *Don't hit her too hard.* She looked hardly strong enough to stand upright; her hair was a duller shade of the children's and was pulled back in a low ponytail beneath a knit cap. All three children surrounded her, hugging and asking questions and Kayla sang, "Momma, Momma, Momma," as she dance around the two women.

Van swallowed. Kathy, despite being sick, didn't look any older than Van. And the other woman? Could she possibly be the grandmother?

"This is Kathy Davis and her mother, Charlise Brighton," Joe said.

"Sorry we're so late but it took a long time to get Kathy checked out of the hospital." Charlise looked around the room. "Kathy insisted on coming in to thank you, but I think we should really be getting her home."

"Of course," Mom Enthorpe said. "And we'll have plenty of time to visit after the holidays. Kids, why don't we take your mom and grandmother over to the house, while you get your things ready?"

"Thank you," Charlise said.

Owen took his mother's other arm. The girls followed closely behind.

"Better take their coats over before they totally forget them," Joe Jr. said.

Granddad had already thought of that and he carried his bundle out the door.

Van put her arm through Joe's, as much to support him as for her own support. She was suddenly feeling a little weepy.

A half hour later, Mom and Joe Jr., both carrying

large bags of holiday food to go, joined them outside the farmhouse to say goodbye. Kathy was already settled into the front seat. Charlise stood with the kids.

"I can't tell you how much I appreciate what you did for the kids here. We sure do appreciate it, don't you, kids?"

The three of them nodded, mumbled thank-yous. There were manly handshakes between Owen and the guys. Hugs from Kayla and Haley, until Haley got to Van.

She looked up.

Van nodded.

Haley's head jerked a reciprocal nod.

"Come on, kids. It's getting late." Charlise trundled them to the backseat.

Van moved closer to Joe and he put his arm around her.

Kayla and Owen climbed in, but Haley stopped, then ran back and threw her arms around Van. If Joe hadn't been supporting her, they both would have fallen over.

Van dropped her arm from Joe and hugged Haley back.

"Thank you," Haley said.

"Thank you, too," Van said.

Then Haley was in the backseat, Charlise shut the door and they drove away.

"Did you get all the presents in the trunk?" Joe asked his dad.

"Most of them. We'll take the rest over tomorrow or the next day."

The Enthorpes returned to the party. Only Joe and Van remained in the lot watching the taillights of the car flit in and out of the trees as they drove away.

"I'm going to miss them," Joe said.

"So am I," Van said. "But they'll be back. Owen will still come out weekends. And Haley and Kayla, well, I hope they'll want to do stuff sometimes."

"I think you found a good shopping sidekick in Haley."

"We did have fun." Van had to stop and swallow. She really *was* going to miss them. More than miss them. It felt like a little piece of her just got snatched away.

"You know something?"

"Hmm?"

Joe breathed out a sigh, a sigh that sounded like he'd been holding it a long time. "I think I learned something this week."

"I did, too. What did you learn?"

Joe held her close but kept his eyes trained on the now deserted road. "That it's not the babies you make . . ."

"But the children of your heart," Van finished.

She looked at Joe, he looked at her.

"We sound like a country-western song," she said.

He laughed. "We sound like . . ."

"Christmas."

*Chapter Twelve*

CHRISTMAS DAY WAS everything Van remembered and more; louder, brighter, more festive and boisterous. There were more presents than Van had ever seen, more silliness and heartfelt gratitude. And even when Elizabeth, in Maddy's absence, began singing "In the Bleak Midwinter," it didn't sound sad. It sounded like a promise.

At first Van tried to steel herself, not give in totally to this wonderful feeling. But she couldn't resist. She knew it wouldn't last, but it would always come back. And that was what counted.

When they finished the second pot of coffee and Mom began gathering up the wrapping paper for the recycling bin, Joe stood. "If you'll excuse us, I have to take Van away for a minute."

Van frowned at him.

"Nothing bad," Joe said. "Just a little present I forgot about."

From the tail of her eye, she saw Granddad wink.

"Don't be late for turkey," Joe Jr. said.

"Better change out of those shoes and put on your muck boots," Granddad added.

She looked from one to the other. "Does this entail livestock of any kind?"

Joe grinned. "Possibly."

She turned to the others. Mom Enthorpe looked clueless, but the two Joes were definitely looking conspiratorial.

Van stood. Pointed at Granddad. "I'm going, but remember, I know where you live."

"Heh, heh, heh," he replied. "When's that turkey gonna be ready?"

Joe held out her coat and snow boots.

She took them, but before she could put them on, he trundled her out the front door and into the truck. "Now you can put on your boots."

She pulled on the boots and sat up. "Where are we going?"

"It's a surprise." He drove down the drive and turned onto the road, but not toward town.

"You know about me and surprises."

"Yeah, that's why it's a surprise and why you have to cover your eyes."

"What? Why?"

"Because it's Christmas. Now cover your eyes, and put your head down so I know you're not peeking."

Van huffed out a sigh, but she covered her eyes with her hands.

After a couple of minutes, the truck turned off the road.

"Where are we going?" she asked.

"Don't look," Joe replied.

They bumped along for another minute then Joe stopped the truck.

Van lifted her head.

"Don't peek!"

"I'm not. Where are we?"

"Stay."

She heard the door open and shut. She was so tempted to take one little look. The passenger door opened and Joe pulled her out of the truck and set her down. Her boots sank in the snow.

"Are you losing me in the woods? Do I get bread-crumbs?"

"Very funny. Now get serious." He turned her around.

She had no idea where they were, but for a change she didn't mind.

"Okay, open your eyes."

She did, blinked against the glare off the snow. Looked further afield. "It's Granddad's house."

"Ours, if we want it."

"Ours?"

"Ours, with his compliments. It needs some work. If you don't like it . . ."

"It's beautiful."

"It's kind of big."

"We can grow into it." She took a breath, exhaled, watched the cloud her breath made in the cold air. "Fill it with kids of our hearts?"

"Only if you really want to."

"I do. But let's wait a year until we get these businesses off the ground."

"Sounds like a plan. And since you just said, 'I do,' I have something to ask you."

He reached into his pocket, brought out a small black box and knelt in the snow. "Vanessa Moran . . ."

**And don't miss the latest full-length
novel from Shelley Noble!**

## *BEACH AT PAINTER'S COVE*

**Four generations of women and one
summer filled with love, family,
secrets, and sisterhood . . .**

The Whitaker family's Connecticut mansion, Muses
by the Sea, has always been a haven for artists,
creativity—and the occasional scandal. Now, after
being estranged for years, four generations of Whitaker
women find themselves once again at The Muses.

Leo, the Whitaker matriarch, lives in the rambling
mansion crammed with artwork and junk. She
plans to stay there until she joins her husband
Wes on the knoll overlooking the cove. Her sister-
in-law Fae, the town eccentric, is desperate to
keep a secret she has been hiding for years.

Jillian, is a jet setting actress, who has run out of men to support her. She thinks selling The Muses will not only bring her the funds to get herself back on top but also make life easier for her mother Leo, and Fae by moving them into assisted living.

Issy, Jillian's daughter, has a successful life as a museum exhibit designer that takes her around the world. But the Muses and her grandmother are the only family she's known and when her sister leaves her own children with Leo, Issy knows she has to step in to help.

Steph, is only twelve-years-old and desperately needs someone to ignite her imagination. What she begins to discover at the Muses could change the course of her future.

Despite storms and moonlight dancing, diva attacks and cat fights, trips to the beach and flights of fancy, these four generations of erratic, dramatic women may just find a way to save the Muses and reunite their family.

**If you missed how Van and Joe fell
in love, be sure to check out**

## *WHISPER BEACH*

Fifteen years ago, seventeen-year-old Vanessa Moran
fell in love and lost her virginity but not to the same
boy. Pregnant, desperate, and humiliated, she fled
friends and family and Whisper Beach, New Jersey,
never breathing a word about her secret to anyone. She
hasn't been back since. Now a professional Manhattan
organizer, she returns to the funeral of her best friend's
husband. She intends on just paying her respects and
leaving—though she can't deny she also wants the
town to see how far she's come as a successful business
woman. But her plans to make this a short visit fall by
the wayside when her girlfriends have other ideas.

Dorie, the owner of the pier's Blue Crab Restaurant
where Van and her friends worked as teenagers, needs
help. Dorie's roving husband spends every penny
they make and now their restaurant is failing.

Joe, the boy Van left behind without an explanation, has never stopped loving her. While he's wary of getting hurt again, he also can't help wondering what would happen if they took up where they left off.

As the summer progresses and the restaurant takes on a new look, trouble comes from unexpected sources. For Van, this summer will test the meaning of friendship and trust—and how far love can bend before it breaks.

## *An Excerpt from* Whisper Beach

VANESSA MORAN WAS wearing black. Of course she always wore black; she was a New Yorker . . . and it was a funeral. She'd dressed meticulously (she always did), fashionable but respectful, chic but not different enough to call attention to herself.

Still, for a betraying instant, standing beneath the sweltering August sun, the gulls wheeling overhead and promising cool salt water nearly within reach, she longed for a pair of faded cutoffs and a T-shirt with some tacky slogan printed across the front.

She shifted her weight, and her heels sank a little lower in the soil. The sweat began to trickle down her back. She could feel her hair beginning to curl. She should have left after mass, sneaked out of the church before anyone recognized her.

But what would be the point of that?

When she saw Gigi sitting bolt upright in that front pew, Van suddenly felt the weight of the years, the guilt, the sadness, the—and by the time she'd roused herself, the pallbearers were already moving the casket down the aisle.

She bowed her head while her cousin and, at one time, best friend passed by, but she couldn't resist glancing up for just a second. Gigi looked older than she should; she'd gained weight. And now she was a widow.

Her cousin, Gigi. Practically the same age, and best friends from the first time Gigi poured the contents of her sippy cup over Vanessa's curly hair. Vanessa didn't remember the incident, but that's what they told her. Of course, you could hardly trust anything the Moran side of her family said.

And Van knew she couldn't leave without at least paying her condolences. Wasn't that really why she'd come? To make her peace with the past. Then let it go.

So she followed the others across the street to the cemetery, stood on the fringes of the group, looking across the flower-covered casket to where her cousin stood between her parents. Gigi leaned against her father, Van's uncle Nate, the best of the Moran clan. On her other side, Aunt Amelia stood stiffly upright. Strong enough for two—or three.

Behind them the Morans, the Gilpatricks, the Dalys, and the Kirks stood clumped together, the women looking properly sad in summer dresses, the men in various versions of upright—nursing hangovers from the two-day wake—wilting inside their suit jackets.

The one person Van didn't see was her father. And that was fine by her.

Gigi, whose real name was Jennifer, was the good girl of the family. Except for the sippy cup incident, she'd always done the right thing. Boring but loyal, which Vanessa had reason to know and appreciate, Gigi was now a widow at thirty-one. It hardly seemed fair.

Then again, what in life was fair?

Van passed a hand over her throat. It came away wet with sweat. This was miserable for everyone, including the priest who was fully robed and standing in the sun in the middle of a New Jersey heat wave.

He opened his hands. It was a gesture all priests used, one that Vanessa had never understood. Benediction or surrender? In this case it could go either way.

". . . et Spiritus Sancti . . ."

Vanessa lowered her head but watched the mourners through her lashes. In the glare of the sun it was hard to distinguish faces. But she knew them. Most of them.

"I wondered if you'd show."

Vanessa's head snapped around.

"Shh. No squealing or kissing and hugging."

"Suze? What are you doing here?"

Suzanne Turner was the only person Van had kept in touch with since leaving Whisper Beach. And that had been sporadic at best. She hadn't actually seen Suze in years. But she was the same Suze, tall and big-boned, expensively but haphazardly dressed in a sleeveless gray sheath and a voile kimono. A college professor, she looked fit enough to wrestle any recalcitrant student into appreciating Chaucer.

Suze leaned closer and whispered, "Same reason you're here. Dorie called me."

"And where is she?"

"Probably over at the pub setting up the reception. She demands your presence."

Vanessa closed her eyes. "I suppose I have to go."

"Damn straight. Dorie said if you sneaked out again without saying good-bye, she'd—and I quote—follow your skinny ass to wherever and give you what for."

Vanessa snorted. Covered it over with a cough when several disgruntled mourners turned to give her the evil eye.

"Let us pray."

Suze pulled her back a little ways from the group. She was trying not to laugh. Which would be a disaster. Suze had a deep belly laugh that could attract crowds.

Vanessa lowered her voice. "How does she know I have a skinny ass? For all she knows I could have gained fifty pounds in the last twelve years."

Suze glanced down at Vanessa's butt. "But you didn't. Did you ever think that maybe Dorie is clairvoyant?"

Vanessa rolled her eyes. She certainly hoped not. She moved closer to Suze, gingerly lifting her heels out of the soil.

"A bitch on shoes, these outdoor funerals," Suze said. "You look great by the way. You're bound to wow whoever might be here and interested."

Van narrowed her eyes at Suze. "How long have you been here? Who else is here?"

"I don't know. I just got a cab from the station. The train was late and I was afraid I'd miss the whole thing. Changed clothes in the parish office. Nice guy, this Father Murphy."

Another snort from Vanessa. She couldn't help it. "You're kidding. His name is Murphy? Really?" Every Sunday her father would drop her mother and her off at the church with a "Going over to Father Murphy's for services. I'll pick you up afterwards." Mike Murphy owned the pub two blocks from the church. Mike was short on sermons, but his bar was well stocked and all his parishioners left happy.

Seemed nothing much had changed in Whisper Beach. They'd be going to the other Father Murphy's as soon as Clay Daly was laid to rest.

"In the name of . . ."

It was inevitable that some one would recognize her. As the amen died away and eyes opened, one pair rested on hers. Van stood a little straighter, lifted her chin. Pretended that her confidence wasn't slipping.

There was a moment of question, then startled recognition, a turn to his neighbor and the news rippled through the circle of mourners like a breeze off the river.

Van helplessly watched it make its way all the way to the family until it hit Gigi full force. Van could see her startle from where she was standing. The jerk of her head, the searching eyes. Van stepped farther back from the crowd and wedged herself between Suze and the Farley Mausoleum.

It was a desperate but futile attempt. Gigi found her and almost as one the entire family, the Morans, the Gilpatricks, the Dalys, and the Kirks, turned in her direction.

"Busted," Suze whispered.

"This is exactly what I didn't want to happen," Van whispered back.

"Then you should have come earlier and made your condolences . . . before the public arrived. You can't expect them not to be curious. It's been twelve years, and half of the people here thought you were dead."

Suze was right. She could have called. Warned them she was coming. Asked if she would even be welcome. She hadn't.

She wasn't even sure why she had come, except that everything had coalesced at once. Her staff had been urging her to take a vacation. Dorie's letter had arrived at the same time. And Van thought what the hell; she blocked out two weeks of her schedule, made reservations at a four-star hotel in Rehoboth Beach, and got out her funeral dress.

Even once she'd packed, dressed, and picked up the rental car, she was still deliberating. She almost drove straight past the parkway exit to Whisper Beach. But in the end she'd come.

She'd known Gigi had gotten married. She'd even

sent a gift. But without a return address. Maybe Gigi was relieved not to have to write a thank-you note.

Van had called her once after she left, just to let Gigi know she was all right. Gigi begged her to come home, but Van couldn't, even if she'd wanted to. And couldn't explain why.

How could she tell Gigi that she was living in an apartment with way too many people, most of them strangers. That she was afraid. Hurt. Angry. Sick. For a long time. That she'd nearly died before she caved and called Suze—not Gigi—for help.

Gigi had already done enough. Cleaned out her bank account to help Van get away. Almost two thousand dollars, her college savings—all stolen while Van slept on the train ride to Manhattan.

"I'm beginning to think I shouldn't have come at all."

"Don't worry. The worst is over."

Oh no it wasn't. Van only hoped that she would be gone before the worst reared his ugly head.

"Well, you can't leave now. Everyone has seen you. Besides, I didn't have time for breakfast and I'm starving."

Gigi passed by, still supported by her father on one side and her mother on the other. Amelia was the only one who looked toward Van and Suze. And Van knew in that instant that regardless of the twelve years that had passed, she hadn't been forgiven.

"I'm not sure I can do this."

"You can and you will." Suze took her by the elbow

and force-marched her toward the street. "We're both going. We're going to say our condolences to Gigi. Say hello to Dorie, eat, and then we can leave."

"I thought it would feel great to come back successful, independent, and well dressed. But now I'm thinking they'll hate me for it. I'm out of place here. What was I thinking? I won't be welcome. I know Aunt Amelia wishes I hadn't come."

"She's one person. And quite frankly, do you really care? You've come to pay your respects, and if they get the added benefit of seeing the success you've made of your life, well, good for you." Suze grinned.

Van couldn't help giving her an answering smile. It would be nice for everyone to know she'd survived. That she'd made something of herself. And maybe she did have a few things to answer for. To some people. Not all. There were some people she would never forgive.

She'd left a lot of unfinished business here. She'd begun to think it could stay unfinished, but standing here, being back even for an hour, drove home how impossible that was. Maybe it was time she just got it done.

She turned abruptly and started around the back of the church.

"Hold up, where are you going?"

"I'm staying out of sight until the last possible moment."

"And make a grand entrance?"

"God, no. We're going in the back way."

**SHELLEY NOBLE** is a *New York Times* and *USA Today* bestselling author of *Whisper Beach* and *Beach Colors*, a #1 Nook bestseller. Other titles include *Stargazey Point*, *Breakwater Bay*, *Forever Beach*—a story of foster adoption in New Jersey—and four spin-off novellas. A former professional dancer and choreographer, she lives on the Jersey Shore and loves to discover new beaches and indulge her passion for lighthouses and vintage carousels. Shelley is a member of Sisters in Crime, Mystery Writers of America, and Women's Fiction Writers Association. For more about Shelley, please visit her websites www.shelleynoble.com and www.shelleyfreydont.com.

Discover great authors, exclusive offers, and more at hc.com.